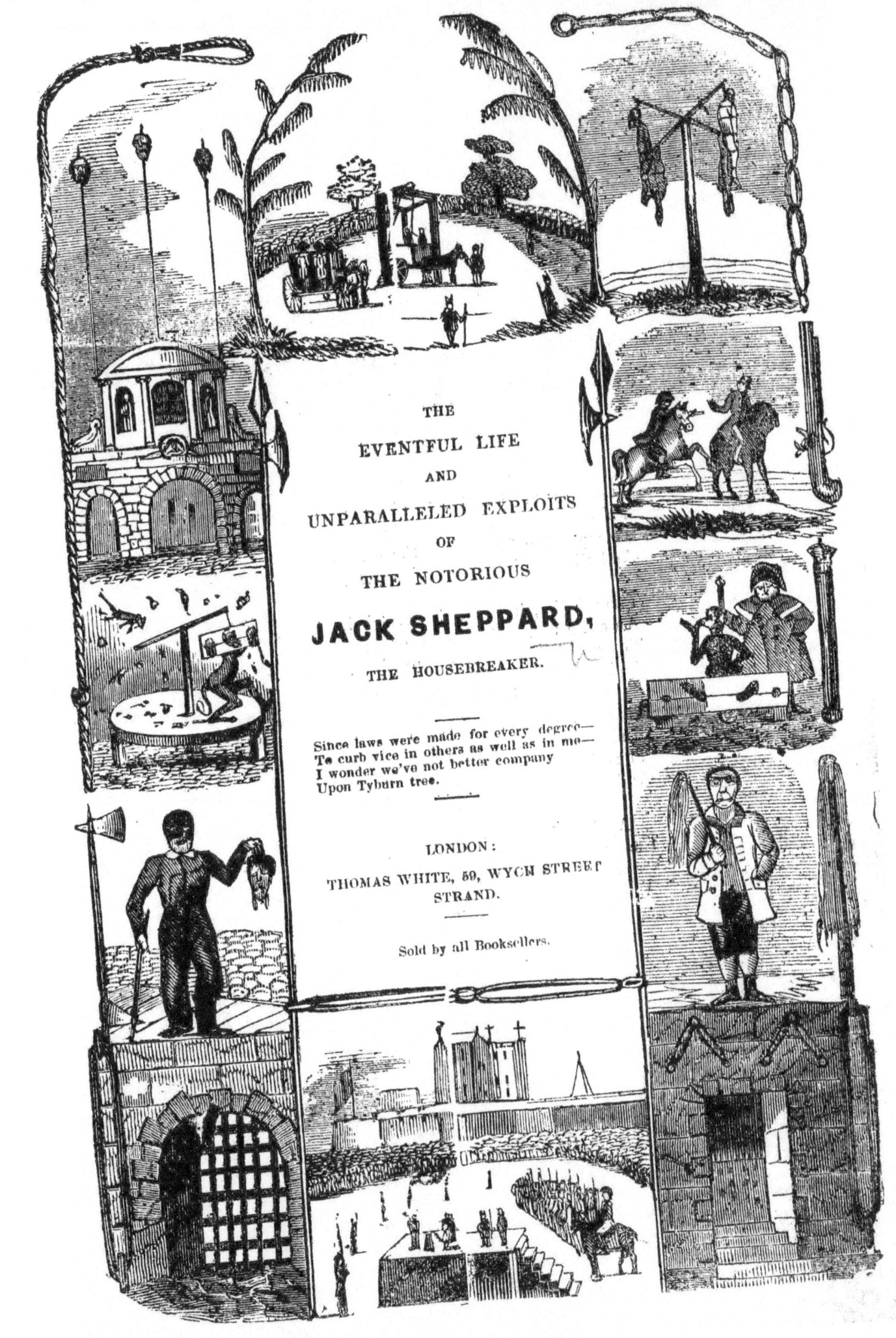

THE EVENTFUL LIFE

AND

UNPARALLELED EXPLOITS

OF

THE NOTORIOUS

JACK SHEPPARD,

THE HOUSEBREAKER.

Since laws were made for every degree—
To curb vice in others as well as in me—
I wonder we've not better company
Upon Tyburn tree.

LONDON:

THOMAS WHITE, 59, WYCH STREET
STRAND.

Sold by all Booksellers.

STANZAS ON THE PORTRAIT OF JACK SHEPPARD,

PAINTED BY SIR JAMES THORNHILL.

THORNHILL, 'tis thine to gild with fame,
Th' obscure, and raise the humble name;
To make the form elude the grave,
And Sheppard from oblivion save.

Though life, in vain, the wretch implores,
An exile to the farthest shores;
Thy pencil brings a kind reprieve,
And bids the dying robber live.

This piece to latest times shall stand,
And show the wonders of thy hand:
Thus former masters graced their name,
And gave egregious robbers fame.

Apelles Alexander drew;
Cæsar is to Aurelius due;
Cromwell in Lilly's works doth shine;
And Sheppard, Thornhill, lives in thine.

JACK SHEPPARD,

as he appeared in the Castle or strong room of Newgate, heavily ironed, handcuffed, and chained to the floor; from whence he effected his extraordinary escape; previous to which he was made a public spectacle—many people of distinction visiting and conversing with him. Copied from the celebrated painting by Sir James Thornhill, the artist to whom the dome of St. Paul's cathedral owes its pictorial embellishments. The stanzas to whose fame, on the opposite page, written by the poet-laureat of that day, are highly laudatory of this portrait.

CHAPTER I.

IT was a gusty, rainy night, in the year 1711, when a woman rather shabbily, yet tawdrily dressed, whose face and figure, though good-looking, displayed symptoms of premature decay from an intimate acquaintance with gin-royal, and whose flaunting, impatient appearance indicated that she was then primed with that nectar of the unfortunate, was loitering under the cloisters of the Temple. The lawyers' clerks as they emerged from their rat-holes, on their way home, or to some more congenial rendezvous, aping the *beau garcon* on a small scale, turned, as they passed, to gaze ; or sporting the second-hand, rake-hellish airs of their masters, addressed her in some commonplace phrase of gallantry ; were invariably treated with insolent derision or slang abuse—the place was gradually becoming deserted, when a middle-aged, well-dressed man of sanctified appearance, whose long-visaged, puritanical face gave outward and visible signs of inward and spiritual grace, entered the archway from Fleet-street, and peering cautiously around him, to see if he was watched or followed, walked hastily down the avenue.

" Am I to be kept waiting here in the cold and wet all night, Mr. KNEE-

BONE," angrily demanded the female: "here have I —"

"I could'nt get here sooner, Mrs. Sheppard," interposed Mr. Kneebone, deprecatingly, "you know, my dear, it would not be prudent for me to be seen—"

"Marry come up with your prudence. Curse me if I'll be treated in this way, unless I have some money I'll go up at once to your shop, I will, and expose you to your fine madam, who for all she holds her head so high, is no better than other folks :—and now Mr. Knee-bone, once for all, am I and the boy to be left to starve—that's what I want to know?"

"Oh Lord" groaned Kneebone, turning up his eyes, and raising his hands, "to hear the unreasonableness of this sinful woman—"

"Sinful woman!" screamed the incensed virago, "and if I am a 'sinful woman,' who was it made me the wretched being I am but you, you old pantile ?"

"Accuse not the ways of Providence," snuffled Kneebone. "If Satan was empowered to make use of you as an instrument to ensnare me from virtue, it was the will of the Lord I should backslide—to be punished as I now am for the good of my soul ; but thou, a vessel of wrath, would never listen to the word—but was ever bent to follow thine own vicious inclinations. As for the lad, I have 'prenticed him to a good master—a chosen vessel—and if he walks in the ways of righteousness, he will prosper, as I have done."

"Don't preach to me," angrily replied Mrs. Sheppard, "you, with all your prudence and hypocrisy, will be found out some day, and as for your chosen vessel, he's got what he deserves for ill-using my Jack ; and what's more, he shall not go again to that place, now he's run away; Jack's got too much spirit to work like a black nigger, and be starved and beat by that psalm-singing brute."

"Woman, you'll be the ruin of the boy, and bring him up to the gallows if you encourage him in idleness and insubordination to his master;" roared Kneebone, forgetful of time and place.

"Ruin, I think you said, didn't you, you smooth-tongued sneaking old wretch ?" retorted the woman sneeringly. "Ruin! you don't want me to tell you, I suppose, who you ruined, do you ? How would you like me to drop in on your fine-dressed madam at home, and tell her that the woman who has most right to you and yours is without a home ; that your child is likely enough to end his days on a gallows, through his father's brutality ? Answer me that, you old fornicator, will you ?"

"The Lord," snuffled Kneebone, half soliliquizing, "chasteneth those whom he loveth and predestinated to fall, has allotted me this trial."

"What's that you're mumbling ?" said the virago, in a tone which caused the smug predestinarian to glance round with alarm, "does the likes of you dare to talk about trials, with every comfort at your call, while I and my child are starving? None of your canting, I tell you, I know you too well, you old vagabond: am I to have my money, or must I call on your marm, and the parish officers for it ?" saying this, the irritated questioner turned away, and walked a few paces in the direction of Kneebone's house. He immediately followed her, and with alarm depicted in his features, begged her to "listen to reason." Mrs. Sheppard saw with pleasure the effect of her threat, and with feigned reluctance stayed her steps, saying, "Well, am I to have the ready or not; yes or no? or I'll be as good as my word, and more besides myself shall know the way I have been treated."

"But my good woman," remonstrated Kneebone.

"Don't good woman me," replied his persecuter in an angry tone ; "you know what you have to expect, and by—"

"Oh Lord!" said he, "what's to be done, the boy will go to ruin."

While Kneebone and Mrs. Sheppard were thus altercating, two men were cautiously approaching them.

"Twig old square-toes, in the corner there," said one to the other, "how nutty he is on the blowen :—what! you old sinner, you çan't leave off your old tricks, eh?" bawled one of them, at the same time shoving his companion against Kneebone. and at the moment dexterously contriving to empty his coat pocket.

"Begone about your business, you horrid villains, or I'll charge the watch with you," exclaimed Kneebone.

"Civil words, you old bluelight, ve air about our business, and shall cut our lucky, and no mistake ;" said one of them; then setting up a shout of laughter, they quickly disappeared down a passage.

The dispute aroused a drowsy old Charley nodding in his box close by, who shot out into an extraordinary state of wakefulness and activity, and shuffling up to Kneebone, he held the lantern to his face, and growled,

"What's all this row about? Come, move on, will you, it's time all honest people were moving home."

Kneebone and Mrs. Sheppard walked towards Temple-lane, but the watchman sticking close to their heels in expectation of being feed to depart, Kneebone had no opportunity of explaining his intentions to Mrs. Sheppard: so, slipping some money into her hand, and appointing to call at her lodgings the next evening at dusk, he wished her good night, and hastily departed. Mrs. Sheppard waited a few moments till Kneebone was out of hearing, and then gave vent in audible, though any thing but complimentary terms, to her feelings towards Kneebone. Shaking the money in her hand, she uttered, "This must do for to-night,

to-morrow we'll see what can be drawn out of the old cull." Wending her way towards Whitefriars, she was joined at the door of a low public-house by a stout ruffianly-looking man.

"Curse it, Dolly, I'm as cold as a corpse, waiting here while you were drawing the old cocksaint, what's thee got girl?"

"I've got but a yellow-hammer to-night, Blueskin, but he's coming over to the Mint to-morrow evening—but where's Nimble Dick and Harry Smart? I saw them on the lay."

"They're inside," replied Blueskin, pointing with his thumb backwards, "they faked his cly, but made nothing but his reader and a lot of papers I can't make head or tail of; Jonathan has got 'em, and he'll make something of them, perhaps." The worthy pair, after partaking of something short at the bar, took boat and crossed the water for the classic ground of the Mint.

Mr. Kneebone, after separating from Mrs. Sheppard in the Temple, stepped into the Devil Tavern, in Fleet-street, for a drop of something to comfort his inward man, and then hastened to his home. But it will be necessary, before we proceed further, to enlighten our readers' understanding with a short description of this important personage.

Mr. Kneebone was a woollen-draper, opposite the May Pole in the Strand, and was one of those sleek, smooth, sanctified, worldly gentlemen, whose religion consists in strict observances of externals; who consider all virtue consists in hypocritically hiding their appetites and passions, in showing no outward signs of the most harmless and virtuous affections, doing that privately which they condemn as a sin when done by others publicly; and of that comfortable state of mind that believes—

"All piety consists therein
In them—in other men all sin."

and consequently disposed to view his own backslidings with a lenient eye, at the same time preserving the balance by the most indignant denunciations upon the slightest slips in others, he was, in fact, one of that numerous sect of religionists who

"Compound for sins they are inclined to
By damning those they have no mind to :"

and very industriously and energetically did he spy, and damn the beams in his neighbour's eye : for, like your very nice people, who must have very nasty ideas, or they would not always be smelling a stink—your super-virtuous people ever have vice in its most hideous form, present to their prurient imagination—ever seeing immorality and wickedness in the most innocent actions, or simple and natural pleasures of life. However, his sedate deportment attracted the attention of his neighbour, Mr. Cheshire, the wealthy cheesemonger and vendor of pork, who thought him worthy of his eldest daughter and £1500. But Mr. Kneebone, previously to his marriage, had the pretty Mrs. Dolly Doallthings for housekeeper, cook, butler, maid of all work, &c., &c. Alas, that such things should be ! but human nature ever was, and will be frail ; and Satan, in an unguarded moment, influenced the virtuous Mr. Kneebone to cast on *the pretty Dolly*

"————A wishful eye,
As she came into the shop one morning,"

upon some household business. Alas, alas ! there's never any mischief done but a woman's at the bottom of it. It is astonishing, when we reflect on the amount of mischief that has been done,—the virtuous resolves that have been melted into thin air by the momentary flash of a sparkling black eye. Poor Mr. Kneebone could not resist ; but, like another Antony, fell. Scandal had insinuated, (but our virtuous pen refuses to repeat the tale,) though Mrs. Kneebone, on taking the reins of government into her own hands, in some degree gave countenance to the report, by suddenly bundling Dolly out of doors, after a jury of matrons at a tea party had held an inquest upon her character. However, all further remarks were put a stop to, by Dolly very shortly after becoming the wife of Jack Sheppard, a rollicking journeyman carpenter in the employ of Roger Wood of Wych Street, who had seized an opportunity of getting acquainted with Dolly while at work upon a job at Mr. Kneebone's house ; and who, worthy man as he was, ever seeking to do good by stealth, advanced the new-married couple sufficient money to commence housekeeping with.

It has frequently been observed of remarkable characters—your desolating kings and cut-throat heroes—that they either come into the world in some unnatural manner, or else some extraordinary freak of Nature is sure to attend their birth, to distinguish them from ordinary mortals. Now dame Nature had determined not to neglect so time-honoured a custom ; and, to lose no time in the production of a hero destined to play so notorious a part in the world, urged on Dolly Sheppard, at the end of five months, to present her loving spouse (much to his astonishment) with a son and heir : but, as the midwife told him she had met with many similar cases in the course of her experience, with the first child, which she attributed to the extraordinary activity of the vital powers facilitating growth, and Dolly continually reproaching him with tears for his scepticism of this proof of her energetic love for him—he, like a good, easy, and prudent man, gave up discussing so abstruse a physiological question, and sat down and smoked his pipe in peace, with this philosophical and consoling reflection, which is recommended to all unfortunate Benedicts placed in a similar predicament :—

"What's done can't be undone, so there's no use fretting about it."

Mr. Kneebone still continuing his kindness to Dolly, became little Jack's godfather; and Sheppard being a good workman, though fond of a little drop, and Dolly a good housekeeper, though fond of showing off the handsome things which Jacky's godfather, and the pretty face and figure nature had provided her, at Bagnige Wells and other places of public amusement. However, things went on as comfortably as they usually do with most married people; and if Sheppard did ride a little rusty at times, Dolly knew how to wheedle him into good humour; or if that failed, had a tongue at command that drove him for peace and quietness to the Black Lion. Until one unlucky day, destined to end their domestic felicity, some malicious person having put some silver spoons into his basket while at work at a gentleman's house, and Sheppard not having occasion for such articles, took them to a silversmith to inquire their value; who, producing a printed bill, and comparing the description therein with the articles offered by Mr. Sheppard, inquired how they came into his possession. Now this person being of a disputatious, incredulous disposition, refused to believe his simple and probable story, and therefore handed that gentleman over to Mr. Hitchin, the city marshall, who happened to be passing by at the time; who, honest man as he was, expressed his doubts to Sheppard, as they walked along towards Guildhall, as to which was the greatest fool of the two.

"You must be very green, young man," said Mr. Hitchen, "to try to sell such articles as these: where you're going to, they'll put you up to a thing or two;—you'll learn on any occurence of this description in future to tell a better tale, I've no doubt."

But the big wigs did not give Mr. Hitchin's prophecy a chance of fulfilment; for it having been hinted to the higher powers that gentlemen of Mr. Sheppard's professional abilities were in great request on some plantations in Virginia, the government generously provided him a passage to the new world, which removed him out of the reach of his enemies; where, modestly changing his name, he became the founder of a family of statesmen and warriors, who rival their ancestor in their desire of appropriating the property of others to their own use; but eschewing such vulgar things as silver spoons, rob a whole nation of their land to get possession of a few ounces o. gold.

Thus was Mrs. Sheppard left a disconsolate widow: but soon drying her eyes at beholding the grief of her numerous admirers, she returned to her old habits and amusements, and liberally dispensed her smiles upon all who had the wherewithal to pay for them; but as time and intemperance dimmed her eyes and muddled her complexion— her reputation diminishing as her wants increased, she resorted occasionally to Mr. Kneebone to supply her necessities; at first expressing contrition and anxiety for Jack, but as she sank deeper and deeper in vice, and became associated with the most abandoned characters of the Mint, she became more reckless in her conduct and importunate in her demands upon Kneebone, who dreading the exposure, (of which she constantly threatened him,) of his connexion with her, submitted with the best grace he could to her demands.

As Jack grew up, he was left to Providence, and such tutors as the Mint might provide, for his education; and as far as it was in the power of his instructors to impart information, it cannot be denied that they found in Jack an apt and attentive scholar: he made the most of the opportunities afforded him, and thus was in a fair way of becoming a finished gallows-bird.

Mr. Kneebone had made two attempts to remove Jack by apprenticing him to a cane chairmaker, in Hounsditch—who, dying, Jack was turned over to another in the same trade, but being ill used, Jack, as has been related, ran away, and was now perfecting himself in "pitch and toss," &c., among as ragged a set of young vagabonds in training for prigs, as could be found in the Mint.

Immediately after robbing Kneebone in the temple, Harry Smith and nimble Dick hastened to a dark corner near the river.

"Damn it, Harry," said Dick, "it's all right now; let's see what's in the reader."

The pocketbook was pulled out and hastily examined, but finding nothing but papers and letters, he exclaimed,

"Curse it; here's a blank: I'll ding it into the dock."

"Come, come," said Harry, "don't try to kimbau me—it's no go: let us have a peep into the lill?"

"You needn't be so peery," replied Dick; "D'ye think I'm going to clerk you? keep it, and welcome, for all the good that's in it. You won't catch me keeping such dangerous things as them about me. We shall do no good to night, and I'm blowed if I an't panum struck: let's go up to the 'Pig and Tinderbox,' and get some peck and boose."

On arriving at the publichouse, they made their way to a back room, dismally lighted by a candle in a lantern hung from the ceiling, whose sickly light was rendered still more miserable by the dense fog of tobacco smoke with which the room was filled. Seated on benches around the room, were assembled as pretty a collection of scoundrels as the moon e'er shone upon; from the sneaking mat macer to the bold rum padder—duffers, swaddlers, fawney coves, funkers and bunters, and other members of those interesting professions, who prefer levying contributions on the property of others, to honestly earning it by their own industry.

In the centre of the room, a mumming cove was amusing the select company with a morris dance. Shoving him unceremoniously aside, much to the landlord's displeasure, who was looking on, they made their way to a vacant corner.

"Here old Bung, bring a tankard of belch, and flick us some panea and casau, and, d'ye hear, hang it up."

"You're not agoing to ligate the candle again, my pippin; it won't fit; so tip up, or bing."

"Why, what screw's loose now, old bottlehead? When did I come the sans prisado rig? Did I ever bilk you, you lumber cove?"

"It's no use trying it on:—once bit twice shy," replied the landlord.

Flinging down the money with a contemptuous air, as if offended at his honour being questioned, they sat down to overhaul the pocketbook.

"What have we here?" said Dick, drawing out some tracts and reading their titles, "'Black Prelacy,' by Smite Bishop Green:—'Hooks and eyes,' for Unbeliever's Breeches." Here's something though," continued he, untying a piece of tape. Nothing, however, presented itself save some letters, which (not having troubled the schoolmaster in their youth,) they were unable to comprehend.

"This is a bad spec," said Harry, "curse the old pantile, I would not have taken the trouble to frisk his cly, if I hadn't made sure of a better haul. Here—damn his tracts, chuck 'em behind the fire."

"Better keep them till Jonathan comes," said Blueskin; "he'll be his rounds shortly: he'll make something on 'em, I'll warrant."

"Well, it's no use being down in the mouth, Dick, so moisten your chaffer, said Harry, handing him the pot. "Well, here's better luck next time: curse it though, this is damned queer-lap. I say, my old bluffer, what d'ye call this? This won't do among friends."

"What won't do, Mistir Dick; what's the matter now?" said the landlord.

"Why, this is the matter. This is cursed queer gatter, my rum bodick—brewed at the rate of a peck of malt to a butt of Thames: dead as a corpse, too—paugh!"

Captain Hamilton and Mrs. Kneebone awkwardly interrupted by the unexpected return
of her husband.—See page 13.

"You're allus finding fault with something," observed the landlord; "if you don't like it, leave it, that's my maxum; your room's at any time better nor yer company."

"You're werry nice to a shade about what company yer keeps, a'nt yer," said a cadger seated in the chimney corner, "yer'll be 'shamed o' me next, I s'pose."

"Ha, ha, ha,—Ho, ho, ho," shouted a dozen voices from different parts of the room, desirous of annoying the landlord and provoking a shindy.

"And when I pays I likes to have my penn'orth, and what's more, while I have the corianders I will, and no

mistake. Put that in yer pipe, and try how yer likes the flavor, my screwbado," replied Harry.

"Come, come, Mister Harry, go slow; the sooner you tops yer boom the better I shall like it; I'll have no bobbery here,—this is no booth," said the landlord.

"This no booth!" sneered Harry, "you lie, you lumber cove, don't yer get yer living on the cross, like us?— when you takes St. Sepulchre's out o' winding some morning, it won't be for yer honesty."

"Give me none of your gum," interrupted the incensed landlord, "or by hell, I'll have you out of that; and sharp's the word, and if you don't keep a civil tongue in your head, I know how to make you."

" And how will you make me? you snivelling pimp?" exclaimed Harry. "If I had you across the water I'd make you tell a different story, I would."

" What's come o' the kinchin, you had here from the country? you crimping bluffer?" screeched out a virago, addressing the landlord.

" Go it Tawny Bess," roared out several of the party.

Livid with passion, the baited landlord turned to his fresh assailant, but knowing the formidable character of the lady, he prudently smothered his resentment, and the volley of abuse that had risen to his tongue, and merely said, " I've nothing to say to you, Mrs. Snacks, so mind your own business. Harry has done me out of the dimmock before, and now comes here to bully me out of it; but I'll make him shell out what he owes me, or I'll let him into a secret before I've done with him."

" And I'll fetch you a click in the gob, if you says again I burnt the ken," replied Harry.

" Cut bene—Cheese it," now interposed several of the bystanders; when the landlord seeing that many of his friends and servants were now ready to take his part, continued, " Draw it mild, my tulip, or I'll be down on your tibby: I knows who wants you—you're worth yer weight at the Old Bailey, you know, and it won't be long before you and the craping curl becomes acquainted."

" You knows who wants me, does yer," said Harry, " you'll blow the gab on me next, I s'pose, you black spy: for deux wins I'd slit that ugly weasand, and save the nubbing cove a job."

Drawing his knife, Harry menacingly approached the landlord, who, seizing a huge painted constable's staff that hung within the bar, rushed out, and aiming a blow at the head of Harry,

would have settled the quarrel at once, had it not been dexterously parried by the crutch of an old beggar.

" Come out, you thief," roared the exasperated landlord, " or by hell I'll have you out;" and seizing Harry by the throat, a desperate struggle commenced.

" Ha, ha, here's a lark. Douse the glims; dab the jigger;" roared out a dozen voices; and the lantern was smashed with a blow from a stick, leaving the combatants in darkness.

" Loose yer hold of my throat, or I'll drive my chiv into you," gasped Harry, who having thrown the landlord, was struggling with him on the floor.

" Give it him, Harry, he's got no friends," shouted Nimble Dick.

While the row was at the highest, amidst the deep curses of the men and shrill yells of the women, the door was suddenly burst open, and the figure of a stout man, armed to the teeth, appeared in the doorway, attended by several men with long poles and lanterns.

" Hollo! what in the devil's name are you about here? Are you all gone mad? Bring a light here, Abraham," exclaimed the new comer, in an authoritative voice. " Is this the way you try to get the traps among ye? Is the hemp too long a growing for you, you gallows birds, that you make your best friends obliged to put the stopper on your crazy doings? What's in the wind now, Jack Hicks?" said the stranger, addressing the landlord.

At the first sound of the strangers voice, the belligerents were suddenly appeased; and the landlord regaining his legs, and swearing vengeance against his opponents, dealt a knock-down blow to the nearest—a poor cripple, who had taken no part in the affray; then, turning to his visitor, said,

" Tis'nt I, Mr. Wild, as kicks up these bobberies, but the damned bullying flashmen as troubles this crib. Howsomever, you're welcome: so tell us what's afloat, now."

" Stow yer whid, and be damned to you, will you ?" politely rejoined Jonathan, for it was that celebrated individual. " Tawney Bess," said he, " I want that watch you prigged from the lushy swell last night.—Come, hand it over, —there's a devil of a row about it ; so I must have it—to oblige a friend."

" I know nuffin of it," sulkily replied the lady.

" Then I'll very soon find a way to make you remember, you lying bunter."

" Well, and if I did take it," said Bess, " I will keep it ; I'm not a going to be done out o' my haul. If you want one, go out and take one, and don't lazily think to fatten yourself with the gains of other people."

" Oh, very well ; if you won't recollect who are your friends, we must try another plan," returned Jonathan. " Hitchin has got a fastener for you, my darling."

" Lord, Mr. Wild ! don't be so hard upon me : I've lumbered the ticker for two quid—it's worth £20 ; here's the ticket."

" Well, that's a sensible girl," said Jonathan ; " I'll see and make it all right, Bess."

" I say, Mr. Powell," he continued, recognising a youth who modestly seeming desirous of avoiding observation, had ensconced himself in a corner, " you'd better call upon me in the morning, or you'll find the air on this side the water disagreeable for your complaint. How is it I hav'nt seen you before ?"

At this moment Jonathan's eye was caught by a signal from Harry Smart, and the thief-taker having exchanged a nod of recognition, walked into the passage : they were soon in deep conversation.

" I'm out o' luck to-night," said Smart, handing the pocketbook to Wild. " Blueskin guv us the office that the old cull, that keeps his woman, would meet her to-night in the Temple, and there

was a rum cly ; but the reader holds nothing but methody tracts and letters."

Taking the pocketbook, Jonathan turned on one side to where a lamp hung against the wall, and proceeded to inspect the letters. A gleam of satisfaction shot across his face as he detected the nature of the correspondence, and the possibility of making a rich harvest of the contents.

" The old buffer will come down pretty handsomely to get these back," soliloquised Jonathan : " and there's matter here, (pocketing the book) if I play my cards right, will make me—" He turned to Smart, carelessly observing, " You've drawn a blank here, Harry— but I shall want you and Dick to-morrow." Then giving some directions to his satellites, who departed, he whispered something to Blueskin, and in company with Abraham and Riddlesden, hastily left the house. Making his way to the Old Bailey, where he had a private lodging, Jonathan sat himself down to attentively peruse the letters. Having satisfied himself as to their contents, he handed them to Riddlesden, and desired him to make a facsimile copy of them. Then musing for a few minutes, he hastily exclaimed, " What if I go myself!" No sooner had he started this idea, than he resolved to put it into immediate execution ; and calling Abraham to attend him, retired into another room.

CHAPTER II.

GREAT was Mr. Kneebone's consternation when, on arriving at home, he discovered the loss of his pocketbook and letters. Like others of the Presbyterians, he was deeply implicated (solely out of hatred to Episcopacy,) in the Jacobite plots for the restoration of the Stuarts to the throne ; and among the papers in the lost book were some letters of importance from the leading men of that party in Scotland and the north of England, detailing the course to be pursued on the demise of the queen for attaining their objects. Having no doubt that he had been robbed of them by the men who shoved against him while conversing with Mrs. Sheppard in the Temple, he determined to pay a visit to Jonathan Wild in the morning, in the hopes, by offering a large reward, to induce the thieves to give it up before the contents of the letters could transpire. Not being expected home so early, Mrs. Kneebone had seized the opportunity of giving a petit souper, and enjoying a tete-a-tete with her admirer, Captain Hamilton, a Jacobite hanger-on of the Court, who, through Kneebone's commercial connexions, secretly corresponded with the partisans of the Stuarts in the North, and who, when not occupied with the graver duties of his mission, killed the time with a little flirtation with the woollen-draper's pretty wife.

Mrs. Kneebone was in temper and habits the very antithesis of her dismal husband—a fat, fair, vain, merry little body; fond of society and gaiety, dying to exhibit her charming self at Court or Ranelagh, where Hamilton had often assured her, her beauty must make an immense sensation—and heartily despising her formal prig of a husband, to whom she had united herself partly in obedience to the wishes of her papa, and partly in the expectation of being, when married, her own mistress, and enjoying those pleasures and liberties uncontrolled which she envied in some of her married acquaintance. But in this respect she had been most grievously disappointed; for her husband, looking upon all such vanities as sinful, debarred her from all amusements whatever; by which sensible conduct he had succeeded in alienating her affections from him, and exhibited himself to her eyes as a detestible domestic tyrant.

Sooth to say, the better half of the puritanical woollen-draper was indeed a very woman, and without any definite intention of evil, she had, from pure love of admiration, and a hope of finding favour in the eyes of the gallant soldier, drawn from their depositories all those aids to personal attraction a pretty female so well understands. Her dress consisted of a richly quilted petticoat, of lustrous and durable silk—of a stoutness which might shame the flimsy fabrics of our modern manufacture. It had erst figured in the train of beauty of the court of Louis Quatorze, and now, curtailed of its flowing majesty, it covered, without concealing, the neat contour of Mrs. Kneebone. Her pretty feet were encased in high heeled shoes of cloth of silver; and though, by "the altitude of a chopine nearer heaven," these vanities of worldly gear had evidently called the blood of their wearer into a rapidity of circulation rather calculated to lead, as Tom Moore ambiguously phrases it—

"The other way, the other way."

Her head was not, however, disfigured with the full-dress abomination of powder; but exhibited her glossy and luxuriant hair in that elegant arrangement we so much admire in the beauties of Sir Peter Lely. A triangular stomacher, while it compressed and set off to advantage the slenderness of her waist and rounded figure, exhibited above it her heaving bosom, suffused with a glow, rivalled only by the bloom of her soft cheek. To such a woman, at the period of Mr. Kneebone's interview with Mrs. Sheppard, was the gallant Captain Hamilton whispering soft nothings. How dangerous such pastimes must be it needs no ghost to tell. Their conversation, at length, naturally glided into a confidential whisper on the subject uppermost in the mind of the lady, viz. her matrimonial connexion. That a tone of querulousness should pervade her speech when dilating on such a topic, will surprise none.

"And how," whispered the insinuating son of Mars, "could so much loveliness wed with such a—"

"Hush!" exclaimed the lady in any

thing but a tone of anger, "I must not listen to any improper conversation regarding my husband: Mr. Kneebone," (laying much emphasis on the *Mister*) "*is* my husband, you know, and—"

"Alas! that it should be so;" exclaimed Hamilton: "Ah! that charms formed to grace a court, should be wasted on one so little capable of appreciating them! Had it been my happy lot to—" and here the practised libertine looked long and ardently into the bright and moistened eyes of the vain and weak-minded woman; who, not yet wholly lost, cast down her tearful eye in simple belief of what the glozing courtier had so readily and smoothly uttered. Heaving a deep drawn sigh, the wily captain seeing his advantage, fell on his knee, and clasping her scarce reluctant waist with one hand, whilst with the other he seized her trembling hand, in a softened voice, and with a languishing air of intense admiration, recited the following :—

"Welcome, welcome, do I sing,
Far more welcome than the Sping;
He that parteth from you never,
Shall enjoy a Spring for ever.

He that to your voice is near,
Breaking from its ivory pale,
Need not walk abroad to hear
The delightful nightingale.

He that looks still in your eyes,
Though the Winter have begun
To benumb our arteries,
Shall not want the Summer sun.

He that still may see your cheeks,
Where all rareness still reposes;
Is a fool, if e'er he seeks
Other lilies, other roses.

He to whom your soft cheek yields,
And perceives your breath in kissing,
All the odours of the fields,
Never, never shall be missing.

He that question would anew,
What fair Eden was of old,
Let him rightly study you,
And a brief of that behold."

"Could I but hope" continued the captain, "for a place in your affections

—but no!—could you think one so unworthy of—"

At this moment the door of the apartment opened, and displayed to the astonished pair the figure of Kneebone, riveted to the spot with astonishment. The captain started to his feet; and, laying his hand on his sword, stood irresolute, though with a look of defiance at the unwelcome intruder. Forgetful of her sex's finesse, Mrs. Kneebone threw herself at the feet of Hamilton, and clasping his knees, entreated him to sheathe his weapon; then recovering her presence of mind, she turned to Kneebone, whose quivering lip and pale cheek bespoke the conflict between his apprehensions and indignation; and exclaimed, as if it was from *his* resentment she feared violence,

"Oh, my dear Stephen;" then throwing herself into his arms, heaving a few sobs, and shedding a few well-dissembled tears, she succeeded in so perplexing the faculties even of that cold blooded calculating old sinner, as almost to shake his faith in the reality of what he had witnessed, and to make him think his—

"Eyes the fools of his other senses,
Or else were worth them all."

Indeed so perplexed was the woollen-draper, that, looking doubtfully from one to the other, he gave the captain the opportunity of recovering his self-possession. Knowing the extent to which Kneebone was committed in their traitorous plots, he advanced with unblushing assurance towards the injured husband, and with courtier-like effrontery congratulated him on his return, and motioning him to a chair, advanced towards the half-astonished lady and handed her to a seat.

With a confident, unblushing air, he commenced with :—

"I have been endeavouring to amuse Mrs. Kneebone during your absence by reciting some lines from a masque which I have lately witnessed; a most exquisite performance. I am really quite astonished at what Mrs. Kneebone has been telling me—that she has never been to a theatre, nor even to a masquerade at Ranelagh." Turning to Mrs. Kneebone, he continued:—" You can have no idea, Madam, what a heavenly place it is. Were it graced by your presence, Paradise itself could not be compared with it."

" Indeed, Mr. Kneebone," began his better half, determined to put her spouse on his defence by commencing the attack herself, " it is really a shame that I should be debarred all the amusements that other ladies are allowed ! There is Mrs. Gadabout; her husband allows her a sedan, and she has frequently pressed me to accompany her to—"

" May I be damned, Madam, if you go," exclaimed Kneebone in a furious rage, forgetful of his assumed character; and ejaculating a round of blasphemies which the reader, without being over pious, might be offended at seeing repeated, he consigned Ranelagh, the theatres, Mrs. Gadabout and her sedan, to a place not to be mentioned to ears polite, but where, according to the best authorities, water is scarce.

" Very well," replied Mrs. Kneebone, with an hysterical sort of laugh, " the world shall know how barbarously I am treated by such a villain ! I tell you once for all, Mr. Kneebone, I have made an appointment with Mrs. Gadabout who will take me to Ranelagh to-morrow, and I shall not break my engagement."

" A good wife, Madam," replied Kneebone, " would keep no company which made her husband uneasy."

" You might have found one of those *good* wives, sir, if you had pleased; I had no objection to it," retorted Mrs. Kneebone.

" I hoped to have found one in you," said Kneebone.

" You did ? I am very much obliged to you for thinking me so poor-spirited a creature, but I hope to convince you

to the contrary. I'm not the silly, senseless girl you took me for," retorted the lady.

" No matter what I took you for," retorted Kneebone bitterly, " I have taken you for better and for worse."

" And at your own desire too, for I am sure you never had mine," said his spouse, with increased acerbity—" I should'nt have broken my heart if Mr. Kneebone had thought proper to bestow himself on any other less beautiful or more happy woman!—ha ! ha ! ha !"

" I hope, madam, you don't imagine that not to have been in my power, or that I married you out of any kind of necessity," muttered Mr. Kneebone.

Mrs. Kneebone, in high indignation at the somewhat sarcastic reply of her liege lord, contemptuously observed, " O, no, sir, I am convinced there are silly women enough ; and far be it from me to accuse *you* of any necessity for a wife. I believe *you* could have been very well contented with the state of a bachelor ; I have no reason to complain of your necessities ; but that, you know, a woman can not tell beforehand."

" I cannot guess what you would insinuate, Mrs. Kneebone : I believe no woman ever had less reason to complain of her husband's want of fondness."

" Then some, I am certain, have great reason to complain of the price they give for them," continued Mrs Kneebone, " but it is useless your pretending to deny it : I have found you out, you base man ! I have discovered your correspondence with that infamous hussey : I know very well how you have been employed this evening : and I have no wishes which unbecome a virtuous woman : no, nor shouldn't if I had married for love, and especially now, when nobody, I am sure, can suspect me of any such thing—"

" And if you did not marry for love, why did you marry, madam?" inquired Kneebone.

" Why—because it was convenient,

and my parents forced me," replied the lady.

"I hope madam, at least, you will not tell me to my face that you have made a convenience of me," said Kneebone.

"I have made nothing of you," replied his wife, " nor do I desire the honour of making anything of you."

" Yes, you have made a husband of me," vociferated Kneebone.

" No;" replied his wife, " you made yourself so : for I repeat once more, it was not my desire, but your own."

"And you should think yourself obliged to me for that desire," angrily interposed Kneebone.

"Ha, sir ! you was not so singular in it," sneered the lady—" I was not in despair. I have had other offers, and better too, in my eyes."

" I wish, then, with all my heart, you had accepted them," replied her husband.

" And I must tell you, Mr. Kneebone, this is a very brutish manner of treating your affectionate wife, to whom you owe such obligations : but I know how to despise it, and to despise you, too, for showing it me. Indeed, I am well enough paid for the foolish preference I gave you: I flattered myself I should, at least, have been used with good manners. I thought I had married a gentleman; but I find you every way contemptible, and below my concern. I will—I will go home. I'll no longer be treated thus by a monster. I despise a villain, who has no regard for me."

The latter part of the speech was delivered amid a cataract of tears and hysterical sobs, and concluded by the lady flinging herself back in her chair and favouring her hearers with a succession of screams, which quickly brought all the household to her assistance ; and last, not least, the pert Mistress Janet, her maid, who had been enjoying a little bit of flirtation at the door with Nicholas Leashballs, the pawnbroker's assistant, who lived next door. During the whole of this dialogue matrimonial,

though it savoured very little of the sweets of matrimony, the captain had been busily, though silently, discussing the contents of a long-necked bottle, apparently perfectly undisturbed by the Jeremiade. Bearing in mind the good grammatical rule—

" When man and wife at odds fall out,
    Let Syntax be your tutor ;
    'Twixt masculine and feminine,
    What should one be but neuter,"—

he prudently abstained from interfering, considering it was a very pretty quarrel as it stood, and knowing it would end, as all such wars of words between husband and wife usually do, in the lady getting the better. Meanwhile, Janet was busily engaged in soothing and restoring her mistress ; alternating her attention to her, with looks of anger and contempt towards her master, and interlarding her discourse with " the old frump; I can't abide such stiff-rumped people :—let me beg of you, ma'am, to retire. Poor soul! the monster ! how can he ill-use so good a lady."

" Silence, woman !" at length roared out Kneebone—goaded to madness by her taunts ; " if your lady sets at defiance my inclinations, the—"

" Well! did ever mortal hear the likes!" interrupted Janet ; " you are enough to spoil the best wife in the world.—Inclinations forsooth ! Just as if a woman was to be governed by her husband's inclinations, though ever so unreasonable. Her husband's inclinations, indeed !—I'd find a way to break his heart if he thwarted my inclinations—pray let me assist you, ma'am."

Aided by the captain, the oppressed lady was just retiring, when the door opened, and a venerable looking old man appeared in the doorway.

The stranger seemed to be a person advanced in years: his grey hair streamed from beneath a black velvet skull-cap over his shoulders, while his long grey beard reached down to the middle of his vest. His dress, which was a long black stuff coat, black breeches, and long gaiters, gave him the appearance of an ecclesiastic, but though the whiteness of his beard imparted a semblance of old age, his bright black eyes which twinkled behind a huge pair of spectacles, his stout limbs, upright bearing, and activity of appearance, indicated a man still in the vigour of life. His eyes seemed to gaze on the form of Mrs. Kneebone, as she retired from the room, with an expression of admiration not at all beseeming his character or years: then turning to Kneebone and Hamilton, and with a keen and suspicious glance peering round the room, he said,

"I am fearful, gentlemen, I have intruded at an undesirable time, but finding the door open, and being unable to make any one hear, I was compelled to announce myself."

Making a signal, which Kneebone and Hamilton recognized as that by which the Jacobites identified each other, and to which they immediately replied, he continued,

"I thought I heard sounds of lamentation, I trust that no misfortune or ill news hath preceeded me?"

"Why no," rejoined Hamilton, "a trifling domestic disagreement between my worthy old friend here and his pretty wife; nothing more. Women have sharp tongues, your reverence, and sometimes 'shoot bitter words as arrows,' and you see it hath disturbed the philosophy of my friend."

"Ah," replied the stranger, "their tongue is their only weapon. Women indeed are the reverse of their mirrors, which reflect without talking; while they, talk without reflecting. At best, their words are but idle wind which passeth."

Gazing intently on Kneebone's ill-shapen hull, and elongated, leather like, mortified phisog., he whispered to Hamilton, "And is yonder lovely creature the wife of that superannuated piece of lumber?" Hamilton laughed assent: and, without any appearance of surprise at the nature of the remark—knowing the contempt in which the Roman Catholic Jacobites held their Presbyterian allies, and the laxity of their morals—merely said—"I see, father, you are a man of taste—so, before we commence business, I am sure you will not refuse a glass of wine. Come, Kneebone, cheer up, man; your lady will be all smiles and sunshine to-morrow:—women's anger is but an April storm. So, fill your glass, and join us in singing."

'The tottering prelates with their trumpery all,
Shall moulder down like elder from the wall."

Kneebone, half stupified by the annoying events of the evening, mechanically drew his chair to the table, and was soon deeply engaged in earnest conversation with the stranger. Artfully paying great deference to the opinions of Kneebone, and covertly joining with Hamilton in laughing at his host, their guest so entirely gained their confidence, that believing him to be what he represented himself, from his apparent intimate knowledge of their secrets, and the important and desired intelligence he pretended to communicate from the court of France, he found no difficulty, after well pushing the bottle, in worming from them all the information he desired of the whole of the plans and persons of the Jacobite leaders.

Their conversation would have furnished a philosophic listener with a curious train of reflection on the easiness with which the most cunning conspirators may be deluded, and how, when once anxiously engaged in a dangerous enterprise, "allowing the wish to become the father to the thought," they, like drowning men who catch at straws, are ready even at the peril of their most cherished hopes—nay, the risk of their existence—to hail every accession of strength of numbers, however con-

Mr. Kneebone consulting with Jonathan Wild how to regain the stolen Pockethook.—See page 18.

temptible with unhesitating confidence. Thus was their wily visitor, by a few well-timed, mysterious, acquiescent nods, where ignorant of their plans, and some energetic declarations of sympathy, and determination of purpose to assist them in their views, enabled to worm from them the secret they thought so well and cunningly guarded. So skilfully did he practise on their credulity, that, ere the morning dawned, not only had he pumped out of them their inmost sentiments, but he had acquired a' thorough knowledge of every plan of the Jacobite leaders, and made himself master of the names, the wealth, the rank, the influence, the residences, and in a few of the more important instances, the very personal appearance of the principal complotters against what they contemptuously designated the "Turnip-seed of Hanover." Pleading indisposition, the newly-arrived Jesuit cautiously shirked his glass, and urging

his ill health as a plea for departure to his lodging, he took his leave ; not, however, before he had obtained from Captain Hamilton a letter of introduction to the head of an influential Catholic family in the north, while from Kneebone he also contrived to extract a short note to a brother traitor at York.

The morning was cold and raw as the stranger issued, with apparent caution, from the house of Kneebone—accompanied by the hearty good wishes of the gay cavalier, and the prudent cautions of the puritanical spy. Turning hastily up one of the obscure courts leading towards Drury Lane, the seeming Jesuit, drawing his cloak around him, pursued his way in thoughtful silence. On arriving at White Hart Yard, he suddenly stopped, and drawing from his bosom the credentials with which he had been furnished, exclaimed with an inward chuckle,

" Are these the conspirators to restore

a throne? Ha! ha! why, they're as green and as simple as silly girls! The vanity of that laced profligate, who, no doubt, calls himself a man of honour; and the double treachery of that hypocritical canter, stand but a poor chance with the cunning of JONATHAN WILD!"

Thus speaking, the stranger unfastened from his head the grizzled hair and beard with which he had been disguised, and thrusting them into his bosom, disclosed, as he stopped beneath the dull glimmer of a street lamp, the repulsive lineaments of that arch-priest of villany. Slowly turning his piercing eyes in every direction, they at last rested on an indistinct shadow, which was just visible at the corner of an opposite turning. Placing his fingers in his mouth, Jonathan gave a low but distinct whistle, which was answered by the form emerging from its lurking place and approaching him.

"Why, Abraham," said Jonathan, "you've had a wait, I reckon. Didn't you think I had dropped in for it with the old Jacobite? But, no! there's little to be got of such. Are you cold, old boy? Take this—get something to warm your old carcase; and, d'ye hear, join me at the crib by nine, and be seen as little about this neighbourhood as possible, and mind—mum."

Thus saying, the worthy master and man separated in opposite directions:. Jonathan slowing bending his steps, apparently immersed in thought, towards the city, while Abraham, humming a flash tune, took his way to some boozing ken in the purlieus of Drury.

CHAPTER III.

EARLY the next morning, Kneebone sallied forth to consult with Jonathan Wild how to regain his pocketbook, and its, to him, important contents. With this view, he directed his steps towards Cock Alley, Cripplegate, where Wild had established an office for the purpose of negociating, for a due consideration, (their value only, or a little more,) the restoration of stolen goods to their owners. A plan of notable convenience to gallant gentlemen who had lost their property in company that would not be agreeable to mention to their wives at home; or to those who had lost pieces of plate they had received from their grandmothers; or to others, who had a particular value for certain rings, watches, heads of canes, snuffboxes, &c. for which they would not take twenty times as much as they were worth—either because they had them a little while or a long while, or that somebody else had had them before, or from some other such excellent reason, which often stamps greater value on a toy than the great bubble-boy himself would have had the impudence to set upon it. He entered a room fitted up with desks, books, clerks, and all the regular appliances of a place of legitimate business. A number of people, who had been robbed, were here assembled on the same errand as Kneebone, and were admitted singly to an inner apartment, the door of which was guarded by a stout man, of singularly forbidding appearance, habited in the cast-off dress of a city marshalman. At length, Kneebone was ushered into the sanctum of the arch-rogue. At a table covered with a cloth, on which were a pair of handcuffs—and, though so early in the morning, a bottle and glasses, sat this prince of scoundrels. He appeared to be a man of about thirty-two years of age, with a broad, low forehead, and high cheek bones. His overhanging shaggy brows, almost hid a pair of little deep-set twinkling black eyes, which, though apparently cast down as if in intense admiration of his buckles, might ever and anon, when unobserved by his visitor, be detected stealing a rapid, yet searching glance, expressive of intense cunning and habitual suspicion. His nose, which was exceedingly short and broad, and at no time a very handsome feature, was not at all improved by a sword-cut, which had crushed in that part intended by nature to be prominent, causing his nostrils, which were broad and expanded, to be elevated in the air, into a most convenient and natural position for taking snuff, to which he continually treated it, from a handsome silver-mounted mull. The upper part of his face and head was short, and the features, as it were, compressed together: the lower portion of his face was elongated to a disproportionate length, while the rapidly receding chin, and fleshy projection of the under-lip, gave an expression of sensuality and cruelty to the lower part of his massively formed head, at once remarkable and repulsive; in short, he looked the very personification of the cunning, resolute, and remorseless villain.

Around the walls of the room, like trophies in an ancient baronial hall, were exhibited a perfect magazine of all kinds of instruments of thievery and violence. Picklocks innumerable; files, saws, dark lanterns, formidable bludgeons, levers of all sizes, from the crowbar down to the powerful little jemmy; pistols, spring-knives and daggers, which he exhibited with ostentation as pretended trophies of conquest, which he had taken from notorious highwaymen and housebreakers whom he had apprehended and brought to justice; though it is quite certain Jonathan did not allow them to get rusty for want of use. But it will be necessary, before we proceed any further, to endeavour to draw the character of this great man, who will play so important a part in this veracious history.

Jonathan Wild had every qualification necessary to form a great man, as his most powerful and predominant passion was ambition: so Nature had, with consummate propriety, adapted all his faculties to the attaining those glorious ends to which this passion directed him. He was extremely ingenious in inventing designs; artful in contriving the means to accomplish his purposes, and resolute in executing them. For, as the most exquisite cunning, and most undaunted boldness, qualified him for any undertaking, so was he not restrained by any of those weaknesses which disappoint the views of men and vulgar souls, and which are comprehended in one general term of *honesty*, which is a corruption of *honosty*, a word derived from what the Greeks call an ass. He was entirely free from those low vices—modesty and good nature, which, as he said, implied a total negation of human greatness, and were the only qualities which absolutely rendered a man incapable of making a considerable figure in the world. His lust was inferior only to his ambition; and as for what simple people call love, he knew not what it was. His avarice was immense; but it was of the rapacious, not of the tenacious kind: his rapaciousness was indeed so violent, that nothing ever contented him but the whole; for however considerable the share was, which his coadjutors allowed him of a booty, he was restless in inventing means to make himself master of the smallest pittance reserved by them. The character which he most valued himself upon, and which he principally honoured in others, was that of hypocrisy. He thought there was little greatness to be expected in a man who acknowledged his vices; but always much to be hoped for from him who professed great virtues: wherefore, though he would always shun the person whom he discovered guilty of a good action, yet he was never deterred by a good character, which was more commonly the effect of profession than action. For which reason he was himself very liberal of honest professions, and had as much goodness and virtue in his mouth as a saint; never in the least scrupling to swear by his honour, even to those who knew him the best: nay, though he held good nature and modesty in the highest contempt, he constantly practised the affectation of both, and recommended them to others, whose welfare, *on his own account*, he wished well to. He laid down several maxims as the certain method of attaining greatness, to which, on his own pursuit of it, he constantly adhered; and as they have been found of prodigious efficacy in various pursuits of life by many of your statesmen, deans, bishops, and others, in their passage to greatness, from Jonathan's down to the present time, we think it no more than proper to let our readers into the secret of rising in the world.

1. Never to do more mischief to another than is necessary to effect his purpose; for mischief is too precious a thing to be thrown away.

2. To know no distinction of men from affection; but to sacrifice all with equal readiness to his interest.

3. Never to communicate more of an affair than was necessary to the person who was to execute it.

4. Not to trust him who hath deceived you, nor who knows he hath been deceived by you.

5. To forgive no enemy; but to be cautious and often dilatory in revenge.

6. To shun poverty and distress, and to ally himself as close as possible to power and riches.

7. To maintain a constant gravity in his countenance and behaviour, and to effect wisdom on all occasions.

8. To foment eternal jealousies in his gang, one of another.

9. Never to reward any one equal to his merit, but always to insinuate that the reward was above it.

10. That all men were knaves or fools, and much the greater number a composition of both.

11. That a good name, like money, must be parted with—or, at least, greatly risked, in order to bring the owner any advantage.

12. That virtues, like precious stones, were easily counterfeited; and that the counterfeits, in both cases, adorned the wearer equally—and that very few had knowledge or discernment sufficient to distinguish the counterfeit jewel from the real.

13. That many men are undone by not going deep enough in roguery; as in gaming, any man may be a loser who doth not play the whole game.

14. That men proclaim their own virtues as shopkeepers expose their goods, in order to profit by them.

15. That the heart was the proper seat of hatred, and the countenance of affection and friendship.

He had many more of the same kind, all equally good as these, found in his study after his decease, for he never promulgated them during his lifetime, not having them constantly in his mouth, as some persons have the rules of virtue and morality, without paying the least regard to them in their actions; for Jonathan by a constant and steady adherence to his rules, in conforming every thing he did to them, acquired at length a settled habit of walking by them, till at last he was in no danger of inadvertently going out of the way, and by these means he arrived at that degree of *greatness* few have equalled, none we may say have exceeded.

By an extraordinary combination of cunning, skill, and audacity, he had formed a gang of lawless villains who recognised him as their head, over whose actions he maintained absolute power, and exercised the most despotic tyranny. The planner and contriver of robberies, he ordained that the plunder should be transferred to him, and awarded them their share; in exchange for which, by preventing surprises, packing juries, bribing evidence, proving alibi, &c., he contributed to their benefit and safety. From his intimate acquaintance with them, and the numerous scouts in his pay, he had instant information of every enterprise they went upon, and the booty they got; and by occasionally bringing such of his gang to justice who had offended him, and his persevering actively in apprehending those who did not belong to his association, he was not only feared and respected by the thieves, but gained reputation with the magistrates and justices, who considered him a very useful man and he was frequently called into court to identify prisoners, which gave him opportunities of serving his associates. But as his subjects were so frequently taken off by untimely ends, his royalty would by degrees have declined, had he not by admirable foresight and care, provided future thieves both for himself and the gallows, by beating up for recruits in the Mint in Southwark; a place, where undone gamesters, broken tradesmen, ruined attorneys' clerks, idle apprentices, loose and disorderly youth, who being born to no fortune, and bred to no trade or profession, were willing to live luxuriously without labour; and being at issue with the law, resorted there for shelter, and whose necessities qualified them for his service. Now having described this truly great character, we will journey on with our history.

In a soft voice, and with affected mildness of manner, like a cat playing with the mouse she intends to devour, but which struck Kneebone as familiar to him though he could not remember where, he desired him to be seated, and begged to be informed to what he owed the honour of his company.

"Why, Mr. Wild," replied Kneebone, "I have come to consult you. Some rogues robbed me of my pocket-book last night, and as it contains nothing but papers, of some consequence to me, though worth nothing to the villains who've got them, I am willing to give a handsome reward to recover it."

"I shall be happy to be of service to you, sir," said Wild, "but you must let me hear all the particulars. Did you see the men that you suspect robbed you?"

"Oh yes," replied Kneebone, "plainly, that is, one of them:—they shoved against me designedly; evidently with the intention to rob me."

"Indeed!" said Wild, "and where was this?"

"Why you see," snuffled Kneebone, hesitatingly, "you know—a—a—I was walking—that is—I went to the Temple to consult my lawyer on some business."

"And what sort of men were they?" asked Wild.

"Why, one of them," replied Kneebone, "was a tall stout man, and had a long surtout coat and apron on. He looked like a ticket porter. The other villain I did not see so plainly, it being very dark."

"And they shoved against you, you say," said Wild. "Did you meet them, then, or were you going the same way?"

"Oh, no!" hastily rejoined Kneebone, (not seeing the drift of the question.) "I was standing still, and they came out of their way purposely to push against me."

"Oh!" drawled Wild, fixing his eyes on Kneebone, "standing still out of the way—cozy fuss in a dark corner, eh?" said he, putting his finger up to his nose and winking hard at Kneebone, then imitating his drawl—"flesh is frail.—Doxy in case, eh?" said he again, treating his client to a subdued and confidential chuckle; then suddenly assuming his previous demure look—"Oh these petticoats! You'll excuse me, Mr. Kneebone, but it's necessary I should know all the circumstances if I am to be of any use."

"He, he, he," keckled Kneebone, somewhat confused, "but you are a man of the world, Mr. Wild;" and then assuming an air of gallantry, he continued "I can't deny but there was a lady in the case. Nothing wrong, though, I assure you. In fact I was exhorting her to shun her sinful way of life; nothing more, nothing more, I assure you."

"Ah! a dangerous and difficult task, I take it, Mr. Kneebone; like taking a Tartar prisoner—eh?—more likely to carry off the conqueror! I trust you've got off safe and sound, Mr. Kneebone! Well, we'll see what can be done." Then ringing a little bell at his elbow, a clerk made his appearance from the outer office.

"Refer to your journal, Mr. Blewitt," said Wild, "and see who were reported to be on the lay in Fleet Street or the Temple, last night."

"You see, Mr. Kneebone, I have a sharp eye on these scamp-feet," continued Wild, "almost every motion of theirs is reported to me by my setters."

After some whispering with the clerk, who shortly retired, he turned to Kneebone, and said, "I think that I know the fellows who spoke with you:—the most expert prigs in London:—nim a man's shirt off his back without his knowing it. I'll tell you a good story of one of these very men. He was apprenticed to a hosier, in Cheapside. One day, when sent out on business by his master, being in want of money, he went to his father's house, and smugged an elegant suit of clothes, he then returned to his master's in this disguise, who did not recognise him, and purchased twenty pounds worth of hosiery, linen, silk stockings, lace ruffles, &c., desiring him to send them to his address, James Montague, Esq., Golden Square, in an hour's time, when he would pay for them. He then went home, slipped off his fine clothes and returned to the shop in his ordinary 'prentice's dress, saw his master pack up the goods, make out the bill and receipt, and, like a young hopeful, went off with the parcel. Can you guess the upshot?"

Kneebone, who had sat somewhat uneasily during the recital of this story, shook his head in token of dissent.

"Why, the young scamp came back with a bloody nose and all over mud, with a cock-and-a-bull story about being knocked down and robbed as he was going across Lincoln's Inn Fields. His worthy master sent for me to advise what was best to be done to recover the goods. I didn't believe the story, but couldn't make anything of it, so I determined to watch, feeling certain that my spark had a pal. One night, after the family were gone to bed, my gentleman softly lets himself out, figged out like a nobleman, and away he hied to Ranelagh. The next morning I called on the governor, and told him I thought I had a clue to the thief. I related to him the last night's adventure, and on searching his trunk we found some of the identical silks and ruffles that had been sent by him to Golden Square. The dumb-founded hosier would not prosecute, so he sent him to boarding-school at Bridewell, as an idle apprentice, where he got acquainted with several like himself, and now is a regular gnostic, and up to all sorts of rum fun. However, Mr. Kneebone, get out a warrant and I'll have the dabs in quod immediately."

"But," interrupted Kneebone, "I'd rather not proceed to extremities, if it can be done without. There is so much trouble in prosecuting."

"Ah, but that's a difficult matter," said Wild; "you see these fellows are so leary, they won't treat, perhaps think it's a trap:—I hardly think it can be done without apprehending them."

But Mr. Kneebone had his own reasons for not wishing to proceed as Jonathan proposed, and rose in his offers at each objection he made, and Wild knowing this, was tormenting him with doubts and difficulties for his own emolument.

"You see, Mr. Kneebone, what an unpleasant situation I should be placed in. I should like to serve you; but there's great danger in it. If it should be discovered that I acted as an agent in this affair, I should be ruined. Compromising felony is a serious business; and now having a clue to this matter, I am bound to bring these fellows to justice.—It is a duty you owe to society, Mr. Kneebone, to prosecute."

"I would rather leave their punishment to Providence, which will, surely, some day overtake them and punish them for all their evil doings. You may depend upon my secrecy, Mr. Wild."

"Unpleasant business, certainly, under all the circumstances, for a gentleman of your character! This is a censorious world. Counsel would be sure to pump out all about the girl. Ha! ha! Well, Mr. Kneebone, I think I can depend on you. To oblige you, I will undertake it; and, if it should be found out, you can bear testimony how unwilling I was to do anything unlawful. I have been cruelly calumniated, Mr. Kneebone; I have many enemies who are striving to ruin me, and I must be cautious whom I serve. Here, Blueskin! (the gentleman in the marshalman's coat popped his head in at the door) this gentleman has been robbed of his pocketbook by Harry Smart and nimble Dick: you know where they are to be found. You must try and negotiate for its return, the gentleman is willing to give ten pounds and ask no questions; but if they are obstinate, I promise them they shall be by the heels in Clerkenwell before this time to-morrow."

"I will give double the reward rather than have any dispute," interposed Kneebone anxious to regain the book.

"Don't be in a hurry, Mr. Kneebone," said Wild, "I've given you my word, and, if it can be done for nothing, it shall; there's no occasion for more than you have offered; I shall have to pay some others, or I would not take a farthing: I want nothing for myself but the good word of those I serve. But I have an appointment with the Lord Mayor this morning: perhaps you will excuse me, Mr. Kneebone; my man will, I dare say, recover your book: —I wish you a good morning."

So saying Jonathan departed, turning the key on the outside, and leaving Kneebone to his meditations within. After waiting some time Blueskin re-

turned, and told him he had succeeded, "Now my rattling gloak," said he, "when I gives the office, just pull that ere pannel, and if you wants your lil, post the cole and take it; and it's my opinion the livelier you looks about it the better. Now then—"

Kneebone understood just enough of these directions to comprehend that he was to pull back the pannel indicated; when a face covered with a black mask appeared: in one hand was a pistol presented at Kneebone's head, and in the other his pocketbook.

"Lord preserve us!" ejaculated Kneebone.

"Damn the dummy!" roared out Blueskin, "what dost see the devil, man? he han't come for thee yet!"

His anxiety to get his papers overcoming his cowardice, he tremblingly deposited the promised reward, and received his book, when the pannel instantly closed. Kneebone immediately opened the pocketbook to ascertain if the papers he was so anxious about were safe, when he was thus interrupted by Blueskin:—

"Now, my Nabs, it's all rug, be alive, and morris."

Overjoyed at finding them apparently untouched, he thrust a guinea into the hand of Blueskin, and speedily made his exit; though not so speedily but that Blueskin contrived dexterously to draw his snuffbox and handkerchief from his pocket; at the same time assuming a burlesque imitation of Kneebone's demure walk and manner, then making a mug, taking a sight, and thrusting his tongue in his cheek, in succession, he turned to the bookkeeper in the outer office, and exclaimed, "Vell, of all the old autem cacklers I ever did see, he's the rummest—ha! ha! ha!— it makes me laugh to think how Jonathan did chaff him about Dolly—ha! ha! What a bite! He's come down dimber with the garnish though, and no mistake!—A husky lour, my reg'lars; this here vipe and the dust bin 'll make

no bad morning's work. I'm walker."
So saying, he sherried off.

CHAPTER IV.
The Mint.

THAT space of ground extending from Union Street to where the King's Bench Prison now stands, on the western side of "Long Southwarke," was, in former times known as Southwark Park, in which was situated Suffolk House, the residence of the celebrated Charles Brandon, duke of Suffolk, who married the sister of Henry the Eighth. The wife-killing king, having become possessed of Suffolk House, converted it into a mint ; but on the removal of the coinage to the Tower, Henry exchanged the house and grounds with archbishop Heth, who, in the reign of queen Mary, of Smithfield memory, sold it to a company of merchants. These speculating gentry pulled down the palace, and erected on the grounds a number of small houses, which were let out into tenements of the lowest description, and soon became, as Stow saith, "the resort of beggars and idle personnes." This colony of vagrants retained the appellation of the Mint, and is still indicated, even to the present day, to the curious enquirer, by a miserable thoroughfare opposite St. George's church, in the Borough, bearing the name of Mint Street.

At the time of which we write, the buildings of this rookery, crowded closely on each other, exhibited lamentable signs of having become ruinous before they were old, from the insufficient manner in which they had been originally erected, and from the neglect of their inhabitants. The dilapidated weather boarding of their gables, clattered in the breeze, while the roofs of many of the dwellings were open to the winds and dews of heaven. Doors off their hinges leaned against the posts, and the shutterless windows displayed many curious contrivances by which

old hats and petticoats were made to perform the duty of glass, in every thing but transparency. In the principal street, which was narrow and muddy, the shops appeared perfect museums of antiquities. In one, old clothes and habiliments of every fashion and age ; here, a shop whose exterior was decorated with silken banners of every hue of the rainbow : there, a den in which the gutters seemed to have been raked for rusty, useless pieces of iron keys, vices, old swords of odd shape and length. The numerous furniture-brokers seemed hospitals for the reception of distressed furniture, full of armless chairs, legless tables, and superannuated chests of drawers ; or reminded the observer of houses on the sea-coast, too often furnished with the spoils of wrecked vessels, as these were probably filled with the relics of the unfortunate : bird-fanciers, tailors, coblers, hat-makers, barbers and publicans, completed the commercial part of the community. The air was redolent with the perfumes of Nicotia and Trinidado, compounded with the savoury steams that emanated from the cookshops, of frying fish, sausages and faggots.

Seated on the steps of the doors, or lolling out of the windows of the miserable hovels, were here and there to be seen faded and painted females, who boldly stared at the passer by, or addressed him in tones of impudent familiarity. Aloft, tier above tier, like trophies of conquest, the windows were decorated with miserable exhibitions of ragged yellow linen, which hung on lines to dry, projected from the broken casements by old brooms, and spoke the wants and distresses of its inhabitants.

The wailing of children, scolding of women, were overwhelmed in the riotous shouts, oaths, profane songs, and boisterous laughter which issued from the alehouses, with which the place abounded.

The Mint had become the resort and swarmed with desperadoes of every

Kneebone taken for a spy, and dragged to the pump.

description; gentlemen who had cause to sing "Fortune's my Foe," here laid perdu till the wheel came round; debtors concealed themselves from the immediate grasp of the law, until they could get their affairs accommodated; bankrupt tradesmen, swindlers, ruined gamesters, irreclaimable prodigals, debauched profligates, housebreakers, highwaymen, and felons of every degree, here sought refuge, and had formed themselves into a community of vagabonds for self-protection against their common enemy—the law.

This commonwealth of rogues was under the domination of a master, who, with the assistance of a council, appointed proper officers to carry his commands into execution. The narrow entrances and outlets to his dominions were guarded by scouts, and had gates,

bars, and chains, which could at a moment's notice be closed upon the sound of a horn, which was the signal when their privileges were invaded by tipstaff or bailiff. On the first alarm, they swarmed out to the rescue as when a hive of bees is disturbed—rendering it difficult and unsafe for the officers of the law to execute writs or warrants emanating even from the highest authorities, unless backed by sufficient force, among men whose safety was inconsistent with warrants or authority, at any time. Thus guarded, they set at defiance all man-catchers; and granted, by a pass, permission to reside within the limits to all who could show good reason to claim its protection; and woe to the unlucky stranger who should presume to reside within its limits, or trespassed on its precincts, without

No. 4

having first paid his respects and garnish to the master, and acknowledged his jurisdiction.

Turning to the right out of the main street under a gateway, a narrow court led into a small open space, which, though not containing above a dozen houses, was dignified with the name of "Mint Square;" in which most of the dwellings were deserted, and so ruinous as to require being shored up, while two thirds of it was occupied by a large puddle of water, decorated here and there with an island of mud and rocks of broken crockery and bricks, on which, like the hull of a ship ashore, laid the carcass of a dead cat.   On a dry portion of this dirty spot two men were walking up and down in close conversation; the one tall, fat, and bloated, who, as he turned in his walk, discovered the features of Jack Hicks, the crimping landlord of Whitefriars: the other, short, stout, and swarthy, appeared from his dress and lolling gait to be a seaman.

"I'll tell you what it is, Mr. Hicks," said the seaman, "it's all very fine what you say, but damn me if I do all your dirty work for nothing. You has good reasons, or you would not be so anxious about sending the boy off. I'll warrant you're well paid for the job, and I expects the same; so don't stand there backing and filling all night: come, out wi' it, man—it's no use trying to gammon me."

"Well, and suppose I have my reasons for getting rid of the brat," said Hicks, "that's neither here nor there. You usen't to be so particular, Captain Johnson. I thought I offered you handsome enough—more than I shall get by it, and you'll not have half the trouble and risk. He's a nice lad."

"Tell that to the marines, my hearty," rejoined the seamen, digging his elbow into the paunch of his companion, "what use is a kid of his age? Howsomdever, I'm not one of yer speecherifying chaps, so say twenty guineas, and it's a bar-

gain if you make it worth my while; and I'll warrant you he shall not trouble you again in this country."

"Could I be certain of that, captain," eagerly rejoined Hicks, laying his hand on the arm of the seaman, and looking with a fixed meaning in his face, "fifty should not part us!"

"Say the word, then, and be certain," rejoined the ruffian; "ha! ha! there's many an opportunity in a dark and stormy night, when a ship's staggering on a wind in a gale, to get rid of a troublesome hand, much more a lad. He might screech like a thousand devils, the howling gale drowns all noise, and the blue sea tells no tales."

"And when will you take him aboard?" said Hicks.

"Why, at once," responded the seaman; "the brigantine lies off St. Mary Overy's stairs. Where is he?"

"Oh, nighish at hand, captain," replied Hicks; "but first we'll wet the bargain over a bowl of punch at the Old Justice—it will be time enough to take him aboard at dusk."

"With all my heart," rejoined the sailor, twitching up his trowsers, and wiping his hand across his mouth in anticipation of the enjoyment. They turned out of the court, and crossing Mint Street, entered a dilapidated tavern, which was nevertheless more ample in dimensions, and less ruinous than many houses in the same evil neighbourhood—where, being joined by another seaman, for the present we will leave them over their liquor.

In a miserable room on the first floor of one of these houses, the furniture of which seemed to have been bought at pennyworths of some of the brokers in the street, without much regard to congruity, sat in deep confabulation Mrs. Sheppard, and—we are loth to confess, but truth must be told, —the godly Mr. Kneebone; between whom, and his dissimilar companion, there seemed a degree of familiarity that would have been puzzling to account for, did not his thick way of speaking, and maudling expressions of fondness for Mrs. Sheppard, lead us to infer that he had been partaking beyond discretion of the contents of the bottle on the table. The fact is, Mr. Kneebone was *muzzy*. Dolly's dress, too, though rigged out much smarter than when last we had the honour of introducing her to the reader, was in a most suspicious state of derangement. Her flushed face, and cap awry, gave indications that the spirit had also vehemently moved her; while Kneebone's apparel appeared as if, unable to preserve his perpendicular, he had been treating himself to a roll under the bed.

"Now my dear Dolly," hiccupped Kneebone, "I will be a friend to you (hiccup). I will be as the dew unto Israel (hiccup)—leave this sinful life, Dolly—ye have ploughed wickedness, ye have reaped iniquity. I will heal your backsliding, (hiccup) ye shall enter my fold—the spirit is active, and loves to inhabit, where it may meet with most work—nay, the worse a vessel is by nature, the more room for grace, where sin aboundeth, grace doth much more abound (hiccup). O, Dolly! we are weak and sinful creatures—the best of us. I have been a sinner myself;" (here the regenerated sinner turned up his eyes and groaned,) "but no man can be wicked after he is possessed of the spirit; (hiccup) there's a wide difference between the days of sin and the days of grace; kiss me, Dolly —there—I will cleave unto thee (hiccup) I will —" here Mr. Kneebone burst out into snatches of song, but as his articulation at this moment was none of the clearest, and he jumbled the words and sentences together, alternately raising his voice to a bawl, and then depressing it to a mumble, very little of their sense or meaning could be gathered but the chorus—

" Wine maketh glad the heart of man."

" But," interrupted Dolly, laying one hand on his shoulder, and with the other patting his jaws, " can I trust you, you are, you know, such a deceiver, Stephen dear, you say the same at home to her."

" Torment me not," interrupted Kneebone, " I love not the woman as I love thee ! O, Dolly, even now my heart yearns towards thee. I have, thou knowest, a little cottage at Hackney, there shalt thou abide with me many days (hiccup). You are a sinful creature, Dolly. Thine heart was lifted up because of thy beauty (hiccup) give us a buss, old girl—leave this wicked place and that fearful man, Bluesky; (hiccup) Lord have mercy upon me if he should come in now."

" O, never fear," said Dolly, coaxingly, " he's otherwise engaged I'll warrant ; but you don't love me Stephen, you've deceived me before," and then with a well dissembled sigh, the jezebel added, " you'll not deceive me again, will you--your own affectionate Dolly—I always loved—" a voice on the stairs prevented their dalliance becoming too warm for the modest pages of this our veritable history. Breaking from his maudlin embrace, the quick-eared woman hastened to the door, while Kneebone's gooseberry eyes followed her in a half stupid stare; the alarm, however, proved only to proceed from a drunken lodger stumbling his way to his attic.

Dolly returned, and Kneebone somewhat sobered by the fright, continued, " Call in the boy that I may converse with him, (hiccup) that I may instil into him the word, train up (hiccup) a child —the way (hiccup) where the devil's my shoe—fetch in the boy, Dolly I'll be a father to the lad, and train him up (hiccup) in the way he should go."

Mrs. Sheppard opened the window, and spying her hopeful son busily engaged gaffing with a pieman in a vacant space on the opposite side of the street, screamed out her command, but Jack being deeply interested in his sport, did not find it convenient to hear.

" Jack, you idle young varmint,

come here, I want you," reiterated his affectionate parent.

"O go to blazes," replied her dutiful son, "you may want then;—it's your turn up," continued he, turning to the pieman.

"Nanny! 'tis by —"

"Damn your heart, you gallus young toad, if you don't come directly I'll fetch yer, drat yer I will, with a broomstick," screeched his incensed mamma.

"Well, I'm blowed if yer ever lets one alone, yer allus wanting summut—well, I'm coming, mother," he sulkily exclaimed, and having by this time finished his game, he slowly ascended the stairs, and presented himself before the revered authors of his being While the preceding dialogue was going on, Mr. Kneebone, overcome with his exertions, had quietly dropt into the arms of Morpheus, and was now playing a solo on his nasal trumpet. So leaving him to his repose, we will describe the appearance of the hero of our story.

His face was that of a quick intelligent boy, with fine hazel eyes, and a clear olive complexion, though appearing as if it and soap and water were very distant acquaintances. His mouth, a feature that more than any other is conceived to display the animal propensities, shewed a strong tendency to animal indulgence, exhibiting a set of teeth an alderman might envy, but would create a suspicion in the mind of a prudent housewife, that it would be preferable to keep him a week than a fortnight; the cheek bones were prominent, the nose slightly depressed, with rather wide nostrils; the chin narrow, but well formed, the forehead broad and lofty, his look full of vivacity and drollery, and seeming to possess a penetration and cunning beyond his years; in short, it was one of those faces that almost makes one in love with roguery, they seem so full of vivacity and enjoyment; his figure, as is usual in boys of active habits, was uncommonly slim, even for his age, which could not be more than twelve, he was attired in black plush knee-breeches, grey drugget waistcoat with extremely long pockets, and a large cuffed long-skirted coat of the same material, the cast off clothes of some one considerably his senior. Walking up to Kneebone, he stood with a demure smile on his features, while his mother by shaking endeavoured to awaken the sleeper; after several incoherent mumblings, he articulated, "tell — m — call to-morrow," at length aroused to some consciousness, he stared with lack-lustre eye on Jack, and exclaimed with a doleful shake of his head, "this is a wicked world, young man, 'the broad path is before you, which leadeth to destruction; give me the glass, Jack—give drink unto him that is ready to perish, and wine unto those that be heavy of heart—now attend to my wisdom, and bow thine ear to my understanding—you're a miserable sinner, Jack, but I will pluck you like a brand from the burning. Follow my example, avoid strong drinks;" here the pious admonisher of youth treated himself to a swig. "Come to me to-morrow, Jack, and I'll make a man of you, here's sixpence—now go, but don't make a beast of yourself." Jack at this unexpected donation pulled his forelock in token of gratitude, and bobbing his head, and throwing out his dexter leg after the most approved fashion of sailors and charity crabs, symbolical of duty and respect, quickly disappeared.

As Jack hastened down the stairs to rejoin his companions, a whimpering sound, as if proceeding from the cellar, attracted his attention; descending a few steps, he listened attentively at the cellar door, and heard a small thin voice half choked with grief, sobbing to be let out. Springing up the steps, he called out to his companions, "Here's a start, here Conky! here's somebody in the cellar;" the boys, with Conky the pieman at their head, hastened to the scene, and listened, but all was silent; at length, after some consultation amongst themselves, it being remembered that the cellar was haunted by the ghost of a man who had hanged himself in the garret; one by one they slunk off to the head of the stairs.

"Hollo!" bawled Jack through the keyhole, "if any one's there, speak." The voice of a child answered "Why it's a kinchin," said Jack, "I wonder how he got there. We'll soon let you out, my kid," rejoined our hero. bounding up the stairs like a kangaroo, with the speed of a congreve rocket, he returned with a Jimmy of Blueskin's, and quickly prized open the ruinous old door, when a fair little frightened boy about eight years old appeared. Pulling him out, the boys clustered around, and began to question him. His story was soon told. His name was Francis Esdaile—he had no father or mother, and he had been stolen away from his nurse by a strange man who brought him to London, and that another strange man had brought him there in a boat about two hours before, and told him if he made any noise before he returned, he would break his bones, but indeed, said he, I was so hungry, and so frightened in the dark cellar, that I could not help crying. The boys listened to his simple tale, and Jack pitying his forlorn condition, immediately changed the sixpence Kneebone had bestowed upon him with the pieman for some food, and little Francis, child-like, forgetting his sorrows, sat down contented in a corner while his new friends recommenced their game.

Shortly after, Hicks and his allies having finished their punch, sallied out from the 'old Justice' to carry their purposes into effect. On arriving at the house where Hicks had immured the child, he descended the stairs leading to the cellar. "Hell and furies!" he exclaimed, stamping with rage on finding the door open, "he's escaped;" descending into the dark cellar, he groped about, cursing his ill stars, and

vowing vengeance against the little whelp, should he discover him, rushing up, he pushed by the seamen, and crossing over in the hopes of obtaining some information of the boys opposite, espied little Francis sitting on the ground. Seizing hold of him by the hair of the head, he brutally struck the poor child in the face till the blood spirted from his mouth and nose, then dashing him to the ground, turned angrily to the boys, and exclaimed, "Now Jack Nastyface, how came that boy here?" "Why I let him out, Mister Jelly belly," impudently replied Jack.

"Then take that, you reptile of hell," said Hicks, bestowing a blow on Jack's head, which though bringing tears into his eyes, stirred up his blood to revenge the indignity, "that will teach you in future how you meddle with what don't concern you."

Our hero retreating a few paces, picked up a piece of brick, and let fly the missile at the head of his assailant, and accompanied the action with "down with the bloody crimps." The shrill war-whoop of the boys presently brought out their companions, who joining in the attack, Hicks and his comrades very soon found themselves placed in a most unpleasant situation, their young assailants pouring on them from corners and positions where their antagonists could not reach them, a shower of briks, mud, and oyster-shells.

"Damn their young hearts," said Johnson, "the sooner we' clear out the better, or we shall get some of our spars damaged, we stand no chance with this cursed mosquito fleet." The uproar soon attracted the attention of the Minters, who without caring the cause, laughed to see the deplorable figure the strangers cut, at length a well-dressed powerful dashing young man hastened up to the scene of combat, and demanded to know the cause of the row.

"Why it's them bloody kidnappers,"

replied Jack, " as hit me, but we'll sarve 'em out."

" What are you doing with the child?" demanded the stranger authoritatively, observing the bleeding condition and frightened appearance of little Francis, whom Hicks held firmly by the collar. " Who has done this?"

" O save me, save me sir, do sir," implored the child, clinging to the stranger for protection.

" Don't be afraid, my pretty lad, they shan't hurt you," said the stranger, then turning to Hicks and the seamen, he resolutely said, " unless you instantly tell me what right you have to the child, it will be better for you to make yourselves scarce before worse comes of it."

" Mind your own business, Mister Hawkins," sulkily answered Hicks, " or maybe you'll scald your fingers in another man's broth."

The seamen laughed scornfully at the implied threat of Hawkins, and roughly pushing against him, attempted to seize the child, but were foiled by his superior strength and activity. At this moment, Hicks drew a knife from his pocket and making a plunge at him, exclaimed, " Damn your blood, you'll find this no child's play, my bullyrock," Hawkins parried the blow, but received the knife in the fleshy part of his arm, which otherwise would have reached his heart.

" That's your game, is it?" replied Hawkins, disengaging a pistol from his breast, " take that you coward," firing his pistol in his face. Hicks fell staggering forward at his feet, at the same moment Johnson seized the child and bore it off, his companion covering his retreat. Drawing his hanger, Hawkins rushed in pursuit, and giving the Minters' cry, a shrill and peculiar cry of alarm well known at the time to the inhabitants of the Mint, shouted, "Arrest, arrest! Help, Mint, help!" To this summons a long loud halloo instantly replied at the corner of the street,

which was answered by the blast of a horn at the extremity of the thoroughfare, and after a short interval by a third, and then a fourth, sounding faintly in the distance, took up the note of alarm.

" The jigger's closed—hurrah, they can't escape us," said a tall ruffian in a butcher's frock, with a red woollen cap on his head, who hastened up to Hawkins, flourishing an immense iron cleaver, " We'll be on the track of the ban dogs ere they can shake the dust off their crab-shells." A garrison called to arms at dead of night on the sudden approach of an enemy, could not have been more effectually roused. Rattles were sprung, windows thrown open, lanterns lighted and hoisted at the ends of long poles were thrust out, illuminating the dark streets, which as if by magic were filled with a crowd of persons of both sexes, armed with such weapons as came most readily to hand, all hurrying in the direction of the supposed arrest, encouraging each other with shouts, and imprecating vengeance on the offending parties. Regardless as the gentry of the Mint usually were of any outrages committed within their precincts upon one another, they were ever on the alert to maintain their privileges, and assist each other against the attack of their common enemy, the sheriff's officers ; and it was only by the adoption of such a course (especially since the late act of suppression passed in the reign of William III. had divested it of some of its privileges as a sanctuary) that the inviolability of the asylum could be preserved, and as Whitefriars and the Savoy no longer afforded places of refuge to the debtor, it was doubly requisite that the island of Bermuda (as the Mint was termed by its occupants) should uphold its rights as long as it was able. Finding their retreat cut off at every turn, the seamen hastily retreated into Wheeler's-rents, a dirty thoroughfare, half street, half lane, running from Mint-street towards St. George's-fields. On arriving at the entrance of a narrow dark entry between two houses, Johnson whispered to his messmate, "hold the entrance, Jack, for a minute, while I force a way into some place where I can stow away this cursed whelp; dashing down the court, and finding the door of an empty house open, he entered, and immediately closing and barricading it within, left his companion to his fate, who resolutely stood on his defence, sword and pistol in hand, as the first detachment of Minsters arrived at the spot, yelling and howling like a pack of hungry wolves for blood.

"Down with the bloody traps," shouted one more daring or better armed than the rest, as he rushed forward on the seaman, who skilfully parried the thrust of the pike, and stepping forward, buried his cutlass in the brains of his antagonist, shivering the blade with the force of the blow. Firing his pistol in the faces of the most forward of the Minters, he retreated down the entry, but finding no means of escape, he fell while desperately endeavouring to force an entrance at a door, beneath the pikes and hatchets of his merciless assailants, who exasperated at the death of their companion, savagely wreaked their vengeance on the inanimate body of their fallen foe. At the first signal of alarm, the master of the Mint who was sitting in solemn conclave with his council, over a huge bowl of punch, hastened to the spot where the affray commenced. Tobias Squintpickle, for so was this worthy called, was a tall "goodly portly man, and a corpulent," whose fair round paunch bespoke his love for the good things of this world, while the shrewd yet merry-glance of his twinkling black eye, in which duplicity struggled with good humour, discovered that though he was a knave, he was a pleasant rascal, a combination of qualities by no means of rare occurrence. At no time a great stickler for ceremony, the illustrious Tobias was not at the present time seen to much advantage, as generally towards the close of the day preferring ease to grandeur, he appeared in dihsabille, in which graceless condition he now presented his burly form to his loving subjects. His august carcass was enveloped in a hairy dogskin vest, and his arms were thrust into a greasy waterman's scarlet jacket, and in place of his coronet of state, his scull was enclosed in a thick thrummed cap, over which appeared an enormous gold-laced hat. Around his waist was tied a small white apron, into which was stuck, by way of sceptre, a short thick truncheon.

Behind this illustrious personage came his bodyguard, consisting of a dozen ferocious-looking scoundrels, with ribbons in their hats, and quarter staves in their hands. In their rear came a horde of ragged, shoeless wretches, bearing blazing links, and lanterns on poles, and armed with every description of offensive weapons; who, as they grouped round the master, kept up so discordant a din of braying of horns, howls and screams of defiance to the bums, that

"You'd swear that old Nick, with Belphagor his clerk.
And Moloch his cad, were abroad for a lark."

"Rot yer, ye roaring bulls of Bashan; be silent, will ye? or, by the poker of Moses, I'll quiet some of you," roared the master, giving a flourish of his truncheon. "D'ye hear anything knock?" he inquired, bestowing a crack on the crown of a bystander, that made all laugh again but the recipient. "Where's the yelper slipped to that caused all this breeze? this is no bum," he continued, as the body of Hicks was turned over on his back by an assistant. "Do any of you know the man? Devil seize you, have you lost your tongues? You could bawl loud enough a moment ago."

"'Tis Jack Hicks, the landlord of the Ken in Whitefriars!" exclaimed Jonathan Wild, who at this moment shoved through the crowd ; " whose handy work is this?" said he.

" That's what we want to know," rejoined the master ; "and as he can't tell us, we suppose, who killed him——"

A groan from Hicks gave indication that he still lived.

" The man yet breathes," interrupted one of the master's blackguards, who had opened the vest of the wounded man.

" Then bear him to our head-quarters," responded Tobias, "while we proceed to look after the others ; for, if my ears do not deceive me, my hounds have run them to earth. Forward, gentlemen of the Mint, to the rescue !"

" Hurrah ! hurrah ! toko for the body-snatchers !" shouted his satellites ; and the phalanx was put in motion in the direction of the affray. At the same time a martial flourish proceeded from cows' horns, canisters filled with stones, rattles and cleavers, which, aided by an accompaniment of barking and yelping cur dogs, produced a full and melodious volume of the most delightful harmony. Inspirited by the martial music, the valiant corps marched in magnificent disorder to the scene of tumult, and arrived at the entry just as the assaulting party had slain their opponent. Listening to the few particulars he could gather from the actors, the master observed—

" Well, this is a strange affair, but we'll see the bottom of it. Outrages of this nature we will not tolerate in our dominions. You say there were two, and one has escaped ; he must have secreted himself in one of these houses." Knocking furiously with his truncheon at the door indicated as that which the other fugitive was supposed to have entered, he demanded entrance—but no answer being returned to the summons, though it was again and again more peremptorily repeated, he seized a betle from one of his guards, and quickly forced an entrance. Followed by his attendants, he rushed in : with curses loud, and imprecations deep, they spread

themselves over the house—searching every nook from the cellar to the attic, without finding a trace of the fugitive.

" Devilish strange," muttered Tobias, " he can't have flown away ; and he must be a sly fox to get out of the Mint without our knowledge."

After a few moments reflection and consultation with his henchman, a tall one-eyed savage, with the other decently clad in mourning for the loss of its fellow, who kept constantly at his side, armed with an enormous flail, he said,

" Paul, it is evident we shall get no information here, so we'll return to head-quarters, and see what we can learn from the wounded man. Over a sneaker of punch perhaps our wits may be sharpened to fathom this queer business."

Giving orders for the outlets to be closely guarded, Tobias thus addressed his troops :—

" Hark'ye, my noble Trojans—ye have turned out like trumps ; and in reward for your labours to night, we'll broach a barrel of right October, to drink confusion to the traps, and success to the island of Bermuda."

With loud hurrahs, the bodies of the dead seaman and the minter were dragged into the house, and laid side by side on the floor, in a lower room ; the door was closed, and with the same discordant music the rabble rout departed to partake of the promised swizzle.

They had not proceeded many yards on their return ere their march was arrested by another row. Hastening in its direction, there soon appeared a band of Minters shouting, laughing, and skipping like a legion of mad devils, around something like a bundle of rags, which they were hauling along the kennel. Halting before the master, they dragged forward their captive, who—raising himself on his knees, hatless, wigless, and shoeless, displayed the form of Kneebone, who, disturbed by the uproar, had endeavoured at that unfortunate moment to effect his escape from the Mint.

Jack Sheppard discovered secreted in the Clockcase.

"Trueno y relampago! Who the devil have we here? *this* must be *somebody* in disguise. Senor me alegro mucho de ver a vm, su mui humilde servidor," exclaimed the master, laying his hand on his breast, and bowing low with an affectation of extreme respect. The worthy Tobias, having in his youth followed the fortunes of the gallant and eccentric Earl of Peterborough in Spain, in the heroic capacity of sutler, thought fit occasionally to display his accomplishments by interlarding his discourse with sundry Spanish phrases and oaths, sometimes

"Horridly stuffed with epithets of war;"

which, if in no way improving the intelligibility of his speech, added much to its variety, and caused him to be looked upon by his followers as a miracle of learning.

A short, sturdy, tatterdemallion, who held Kneebone by the ends of his cravat, here stepped forward. His dirty platter-face, for features he had none, (two holes only indicating the spot where Nature had formerly placed a nose) was awfully seamed with the small pox, and as plainly expressed, as if the words had been stamped on his forehead, the very concentrated essence of villany. Through a wide gash in his upper lip projected a pair of rabbits' teeth, and over a bul-

No. 5.

wark of blubber, peered a pair—no, not a pair, but two odd—pigs' eyes, one of which appeared as if mounted on a swivel, and slued round to all points of the compass ; or, as the master said, had a roving commission. Stroking down the fiery-red bristles that stood out in all manner of extraordinary directions from his poll, like a cane-brake after a hurricane, this interesting specimen of humanity threw himself into a theatrical attitude, and with a voice like a bee in a pitcher, thus expressed himself :—

"Please yer, my noble bos, as I vos on the tout, I twigs this heer queer gil a trying to sneak by my post. ' That's not a 'spectable man,' says I to myself; ' I'll be jiggered if it isn't one of they bloody Moabites—I'll be down on *his* tibby.' So paddling arter him, I grabs him by the scruff o' his nub, and brings him up all standing. 'Vere are you a toddling to?' vispers I ; ' 'vy home, my honest man,' says he to me. 'Vere's your pass?' says I. 'Pass!' says he, quite innocent like, ' I an't got none.' ' None o' that 'ere,' says I, ' it won't fit—yer a spy.' So seeing he vos a furrener, according to orders, I've valked him afore yer emperorship, for to anser any kervestions yer honor likes to ax him."

"And a very sensible proceeding, too, Vegetables," rejoined the master. "Now my kiddy," he continued, turning to Kneebone, " what's brought you to Bermuda? and how dare you attempt to leave our dominions without a pass? Speak, thou ganso. What was your business in the Mint?"

"Down with the ban-dog—down with him ; to the pump—to the pump with the spy," screamed the demoniac crew, as they flourished their bludgeons over his head.

The threatening gestures, and furious expressions of the ruffians who surrounded him; their swarthy visages glaring in the smoky, red light of the torches they waved about—increased Kneebone's confusion and terror to such a degree, as to deprive him of the power of speech.

"Now, then, picaron, porque no responde—who are your companions that have created all this disturbance, and slain one of my faithful subjects?" imperatively demanded the master.

"Good sir," at length gasped Kneebone, crawling to the feet of Tobias— "have mercy; I am no bailiff, I am no spy: deliver me from these workers of iniquity—save me from these bloody Molochs ; take all I have, but spare my life."

"Who are you, then? Do you wish to claim the privileges of the Mint, and pay your garnish as one of our ancient and honourable fraternity; will you pay your footing, or will you taste our aqua pumpaginis?" inquired Tobias.

"Aye, aye; will you post the cole? Come, pour out the balsam, my hog-grunter, or we'll soon square accounts with you," chorused the Minters.

"Oh, oh," groaned Kneebone, beginning to comprehend the nature of the demand ; "I have been robbed of my purse."

"Why, then, old spit to windard," said a sailor, " I guess you're at point nonplus, for you'll get no credit here."

"Robbed!" shouted Tobias, " over the left. A pretty story, truly. Robbed ! ha! ha! ha! in this respectable company too! Who will you gammon to believe that? why, it's a reflection on the honour of the Minters. Be more circumspect in your language, fellow."

"To the pump with the spy—away with him," roared the spectators, who began to express their dissatisfaction at the delay of their expected sport by a sound of impatience like the growl of a bear.

"Indeed, indeed, it's true," cried Kneebone. "This man, who stopped me, demanded money to let me pass ; and when I pulled out my purse he snatched it from me."

"Ha! ha!" exclaimed the master—

I do smell a rat; here's treason in the camp. What, bubble our exchequer! Curse yer, you bracketfaced hound," he angrily bellowed to the gentleman with the carrotty pole—"Who appointed you our collector of taxes? Cuerpo de guardia—seize and search him".

Instantly half a dozen of Tobias' lifeguards laid hold of the offender, while Paul leisurely proceeded to overhaul his pockets, of which there were as many as there were rags. After fruitlessly turning inside out about forty, the purse was dragged from its hiding place beneath his armpits.

"That's the ticket," exclaimed Tobias, with a twinkle of his eye, as he clutched the purse. "Now, for your dishonesty, Senor Romo, you are fined double the amount: one half of the penalty to go to the informer, (I only wish he may get it,) and the other half we shall forthwith deposit in our royal treasury; and consider yourself let off very easy, Senor Zanahorias,"bestowing a kick on the breech of the despoiled collector, who slunk into the body of the crowd amidst their laughter and jeering remarks.

"I say, Carrots," said one, " come to me to-morrow, and I'll exert my interest to get yer into the verkhus."

"Vy now, I dare say," remarked another, "he's saved enough in his place to start vith a catsmeat barrow."

"Lord, vot a shocking ugly nose," sniggered a third.

Kneebone, who had intently watched these proceedings, and had from thence begun to infer, from the expressions of indignation of the master at the dishonesty of his follower, that he had in his mind done them some injustice, and that they were a honester set of fellows than they looked—here put in his claim that his property might be restored to him, and he be allowed to depart. A loud laugh, however, soon told him how fallacious were his hopes.

"Que bestia! Did you ever hear such an audacious demand?" inquired the master of his associates. "Property! nonsense, man, you have none. You're a waif, a castaway, a wreck thrown ashore on our coast; and by all the laws of flotsam and jetsam, your property is confiscated to our royal uses. And now, fellow, you have been detected secretly prowling about my dominions, without any ostensible object, and without a pass; for such offences you have subjected yourself to heavy penalties. Moreover, you stand convicted of an atrocious attempt to bribe our officers from their duty. You are suspected to be a spy, or something worse—a Moabite, in league with some desperate Mohawks, who have invaded our territories, (for what purpose we have yet to learn,) created a riot, and slain one of my peaceable subjects—

"Oh, no, no; hear me," interrupted Kneebone. "I've done none of this—I'm an innocent, ill—"

"Silence, and don't interrupt the Court;" bawled Tobias. "For these abominable acts you have been convicted by an impartial jury; and now have you any thing to say why justice should not be immediately done to you for your manifold transgressions?"

"Justice, you villains!" screamed Kneebone, at the top of his voice, incensed beyond all discretion at this farce, "I will have justice for this robbery—for this assault—if there's law to be had, I'll punish you, you rascals, you scoundrels, you damnable beasts, I'll—"

"Ha, ha, ha!" roared the Bermudians at his anger and impotent threats. "Poco a poco, senor," said the master; "what! dispute our powers and jurisdiction? Listen, you contumacious varlet, the sentence of this court is, that you forthwith be taken hence to our place of public execution, and there be pumped upon until you are purged clean of all your offences, and the Lord have mercy on your unfortunate carcass!"

"Whom the Lord loveth he correcteth, even as a father the son in whom he delighteth," soliloquised Kneebone.

"Why then its my opinion, you old Pantile, you're an especial favourite of his'n," said Paul, "for—"

"Avaunt, thou mocker," replied Kneebone, as Paul proceeded to place a line round his body; "if there's law and justice to be had, I'll make you smart for this!"

"Hurrah! Away with him!" shouted his executioners—"Buen provecho le haga! ha, ha, ha! most potent, grave and reverend signor. Dios le de fortuna—a la obediencia—ha, ha, ha! Le beso las manos," ironically cried out Tobias, as they towed him into the kennel.

His screams for help were drowned in roars of laughter: capering around him, shoving one another over him and bonnetting each other, they dragged the miserable wretch along: his hat placed on one pole, his wig on another, were borne before him in triumph, until arriving at the pump they forced him under the spout; then lathering his face with mud and cramming his mouth with filth, they proceeded to scrape him with an iron hoop, amidst the jeers and laughter of the mob.

"Let's have a look at him," exclaimed Ragetty Moll, planting herself in front of Kneebone with her arms akimbo.

"I vants a husband, I does! Vot a beauty now he's clean shaved; I'm blest if I shouldn't like to have a kid by him if it vos only to guv to the pigs."

Then manning the pump, a deluge of water was poured over him sufficient to wash him clean.

"Vy, yer all in a perspiration, as the gridiron said to the mutton-chop:—aint yer sorry yer cleaned yerself this morning, my gulpin? but never mind, it'll all rub out ven its a dry," politely remarked one of his persecutors.

By this time a large piece of tarpauling having been procured, he was tumbled into it, and twenty or thirty stout fellows, with a one-two-three hurrah, tosssed him high into the air.

"Murder! H-e-lp! you v-i-l-lains, I'll—have—ye hanged. Mercy—O-h!"

While this interesting sport was going on, our hero, young Jack, who for some time had been enjoying the fun, discovered that it was Kneebone. Hastily running to his mother with the news, she rushed into the crowd, and let fly right and left with such hearty goodwill, that the tarpauling was let go to protect themselves from the unexpected assault in the rear; and Kneebone was rolled on the ground. Dolly, planting herself astride the prostrate woollendraper, tauntingly dared the Minters to the attack. At this moment, and just as they were about to retaliate, a reinforcement in the shape of Jonathan Wild, Abrahams and Blueskin, entered the field, and ranged themselves on the side of Mrs. Sheppard.

His appearance was greeted with loud cheers by the mob, whom he amused with jokes and chaff, while Jack was dispatched with a message to Paul, who, sounding his horn, as a notice that the promised heavy-wet was on the tap, the Minters rapidly absconded from the ground. Raising the gasping and exhausted form of Kneebone, Jonathan and his pals bore him to Mrs. Sheppard's, where, by the aid of a little brandy and dry clothes, which Jonathan procured him, he quickly recovered from the effects of the rough usage he had received.

"And now, Mr. Wild," said Kneebone, who forgetful of his cant, felt really grateful fer the opportune aid and attentions of Jonathan, "if at any time it is in my power to serve you in return for the obligations I am under to you, I shall be obliged by your naming it: you may command my services whenever you may require them. I have been robbed of my purse by these lawless villains, or I would reward those men of yours, but if they will come tomorrow---"

"Say no more about it, sir, replied Wild, "you may consider yourself fortunate in having escaped with life from their hands; but stay, on second thoughts, you can serve me, and that materially, Mr. Kneebone; and that is by taking charge of a little boy for a short time, whom I have rescued from death, until I can discover his friends."

Kneebone's face at this proposition wore for a moment a blank appearance, as the embarrassing idea obtruded itself on his mind of what his wife might say to this unexpected addition to his family, as well as its interfering with his designs of providing for Jack. So evanescent is human gratitude, so soon does the heart of man hesitate to incur the slightest inconvenience in repayment of benefits received!

Mr. Wild seemed to surmise what was passing in the mind of Kneebone, and suggested, that as it was necessary to invent some tale for the boy's appearance to his wife, nothing could be better than to relate that he had been nearly killed in rescuing the child from some ruffians who were about to drown it. " She will," exclaimed he, "readily believe that: a woman's heart is ever the seat of tenderness, and ready to believe a tale of sorrow, and commiserate the victim ; more especially when it is a pretty child, it's a passport to her heart at once. Besides, man, you will raise yourself in her estimation by your bravery and humanity, and I will take care to corroborate the story in every particular, when I call tomorrow: but caution her to be silent, as the child's enemies most likely are powerful, and still thirst for his blood.

Kneebone, glad of so feasible an excuse, quickly chimed in to the proposition ; and little Francis being confided to his care, he shortly after, under the guidance of Abraham, set out on his return home.

CHAPTER V.

We will now return to follow the footsteps of Jonathan Wild the Great, who our readers will recollect after the departure of the master and his myrmidons, had remained behind with the senseless body of Hicks.

Having questioned and cross examined the lads who still stood gazing on the spot, and learning from them all the particulars of the origin of the disturbance, Jonathan, after a few moments' deliberation, said, as if to himself, " There's more in this than meets the eye: I must and will pump out of that scoundrel Hicks, the mystery of this child; and if I do worm it out of him---" here an expression of malignant vengeance flitted over his face, " I'll teach him, now he's in my power, the peril of crossing my path." Flinging a few coppers amongst the boys, he hastened to the 'Old Justice', and ascended to the room where the wounded man was deposited on a truckle bed.

Removing the bandages that the bystanders had applied to stop the effusion of blood, he proceeded to examine the nature of the wound. Finding it but superficial, he muttered to himself—" Pish ! there's not much harm done here ; stunned by the contusion, I suppose, or perhaps faint from the loss of a little blood. I must frighten him, though, into the belief that it is worse, or I shall get nothing out of the cowardly close hound."

By the application of restoratives, the wounded man was shortly brought to a state of consciousness, when Jonathan, with pretended commiseration, took him by the hand and said,

" Why Hicks, my man, this is a sad job. I'm sorry to see you thus : if there is any thing I can do for you, you may command me."

" Oh ! Mr. Wild," groaned Hicks, " you don't think I'm dangerously hurt, do you ?"

" Why," replied Wild, " it's an ugly

hole, and it's no use flattering you in a case like this : as a friend, I'd advise you if you have any thing to say, to make haste.   Is there any thing I can do to serve you ;" again asked Wild with an affectation of sincere friendship.

"Oh Christ ! have mercy," cried the frightened wretch ; " it is not mortal, is it ?"   O give me air—I cannot breathe—open the window, I pray—water—water—give me water. O God, is there no help—is there no surgeon ?"

"You'll soon be past the help of man," said Wild, with a significant look ; "you have more need now of a parson.   Shall I send for one ?" asked he sneeringly.

Oh ! no, no," gasped Hicks wildly ; " O God ! I cannot die ; I am not fit to die ; mercy ! mercy !"

"Come, come, Hicks," said Wild, "be a man ; 'tis what we all must come to, some day, but tell me, do you know who did this ?"

"That cursed villain Hawkins," replied Hicks with a look of intense malignity, " but if I live, I'll hang him for it."

"Hawkins !" repeated Wild, "Damnation ! here Abrahams," beckoning to his man who followed him in all his movements like his shadow, "Quick ! seek him out ;" and whispering, said, " tell him to waste no time here, but spur and join Dick Swift at the ' White Hart,' there's better game for him afoot."

Clearing the room of the spectators, closing and carefully fastening the door, Jonathan seated himself by the side of the bed, and said,

"Come, man, if l am to serve you in this matter, make haste ; time's too precious to both of us, to waste, what had Hawkins to do with this child ?"

" Nothing ;" sulkily replied Hicks, turning his face to the wall as if unwilling to be further questioned on the subject.

Nothing ! why something must be done with this young Esdaile ; you don't want him running about the Mint, do you ?" asked Wild, with a leer as he watched the effect of the pronunciation of the name.

" Ha !" exclaimed Hicks with surprise, starting up in the bed.   "How learnt you his name."

"Never mind how ;" returned Jonathan ; "you see I *do* know it ; so now will you confide in me ?"

" Has not Johnson escaped ?" anxiously inquired Hicks.

"Escaped ! no ; that's impossible," said Wild ; " the Mint is up and on his trail ; it's most likely he's knocked on the head for a bailiff by this time, it's a blow first and enquiry afterwards generally with these blades "

"Hasten then, and secure the brat," said Hicks, " it—"

" Not so fast, not so fast," rejoined Wild.   " I'll find him, all in good time ; but as we may not meet again, what am I to do with him, and who am I to look to for remuneration ? I don't usually meddle in other people's affairs for nothing."

" Send the whelp to hell, if you like," savagely said Hicks, " and you'll find Sir Luke Gascoigne, my old master, a good paymaster."   Grinding his teeth, with dreadful imprecations he lamented his mishap.   " I could die happy were I but sure I was revenged."

" And Sir Luke too, I daresay he has his reasons for sending this youngster a trip to the plantations or elsewhere. What relation does he stand to the child, eh ?" asked Wild.

"He is his uncle and guardian," replied Hicks.

"Ah, I see ;" said Wild ; "but now let's have a look at this wound of your's. I will not hurt you, I have some little skill in pharmacy as you shall see."

Taking a wet sponge, and gently dabbing the wound so as to remove the clotted blood, he added, " I have a medicine here, (taking a small phial from his pocket containing a pure transparent liquid,) which I obtained from a German Doctor, worth its weight in gold, 'twill soon ease all pain."

Carefully withdrawing the stopper, a a fragrant perfume diffused itself through the room, then pouring a drop or two into the wound, a devilish grin spread over his features as he watched its effects.

Suddenly Hicks sprang up in the bed; his eyes glared, and then became fixed; stretching out his arms, with his hands firmly clenched, he essayed to speak: his jaws convulsively moved, but no sound came forth; a gasp—another; a faint sigh, and the wretch fell back and expired.

"Soh! fool; you thought yourself a match for Jonathan Wild, and dared to cross his path. Thus shall all such perish. *You!* rival me, and with such an ally as that pudding head Hitchin, ha, ha, ha. Now let's see what you've got about you. Ah!" he exclaimed as he examined the contents of a pocketbook, "clever rogues these; put all down in black and white; excuse the liberty (nodding derisively towards the corpse,) I'll just look over the correspondence."

"DEAR JOHN,—

Hum, ha!—"Exceedingly engaged—leave all to you—rid me effectually."—hum, ha—"place in excise,"—a—a—hum—--"as you value my friendship---be secret"—a—a
"LUKE GASCOIGNE.

Very well. Now am I, with the help of that child, master of the fortune of Sir Luke Gascoigne: so we will proceed to look after this bold smuggler; and if I am in time to save his bacon, he too may serve my purposes: I've a long time sought to meet with him. Good night, friend Hicks; I've robbed the nubbing cove of a customer, but I dare say I shall be able to make it up to him another time.

So saying, he closed the door, and descending the stairs, made the best of his way to where the flashing lights, and the bellowing and howling of these sons of Belial, indicated the scene of strife.

Forcing his way through the crowd in the passage, he entered the house. All within were too much occupied to notice his proceedings, while he creeping cautiously up the stairs, waited silently till the last man had descended, and then unmasking a dark lantern, he ascended a broken ladder into the roof, and passing out of a trapdoor proceeded minutely to examine the tiles as he went; at length espying several that were scratched and broken, and one or two apparently recently dislodged—as the crumbling mortar still laid in its place—by the inside of a stack of chimneys, he closed his lantern, and ascending the gable looked searchingly around. Nothing, however, met his sight. Descending the other side of the roof he proceeded to grope his way: on his right rose the roof, against which he leaned and steadied himself as he made his way along a narrow gutter. The night was profoundly dark, though the ruddy glare of the torches in the street below threw out the gabled roofs and tall chimneys around in strong relief, casting into deep shadow, and thus rendering more perplexing, the narrow and dangerous path he trod, where a single false step might precipitate him into the court below, and from which he was only guarded by a low parapet of loose bricks on his left scarcely reaching to his knees.

On arriving at the end of the gutter, a stack of tall chimnies blocked all further progress.

"Damnation!" he exclaimed, "he cannot then have passed this way."

Unmasking his lantern he again glanced around. A few feet beneath the parapet a narrow piece of timber stretching across the court from house to house met his view.

"Phiew," whistled he, "curse these

sailors! I should'nt wonder, now, if the fellow has'nt crossed that cat's bridge, he can have escaped no other way. At the risk of my neck I'll follow; what one man has done it shall never be said Jonathan Wild was afraid to attempt; so here goes: it's hopping the twig whichever way it ends."

Lowering himself carefully on the rafter, he turned, and after a few moment's hesitation, extending his arms to balance himself, and fixing his eyes on an object before him, he commenced the perilous passage. On reaching the opposite side, in the hurry and anxiety to secure himself, he threw his body forward against the parapet and grasped the crumbling brickwork, which instantly gave way. For a moment he hung suspended. A prayer burst from his lips, as he fancied he saw the face of Hicks grinning over the parapet. The big sweat drops of agony and fear, burst from his forehead as he convulsively dug his nails into the bricks and endeavoured to swing his legs over the beam.

At length, nerved by despair, by a desperate effort he regained his footing, and drawing himself up reached the roof in safety. Seating himself to rest a few minutes, he drew a deep inspiration, as he gazed on the danger he had escaped, and then laughing at his fears, pursued his search. Scaling the roofs of the adjoining houses, with which he seemed to be well acquainted, he approached one whose gable turned towards the others, and possessing a small opening which served for window or door, appeared to be the object of his toilsome search, Drawing and cocking a pistol, he burst open this aperture with his foot, and then unmasking his light, he threw it on the figure of the fugitive, at the further end of a large loft.

"Good evening to you, Captain Johnson," said Wild; "you have led me a pretty dance, but I've found you at last."

"Advance a step, and I fire:" exclaimed Johnson fiercely.

"That would be giving a friend a warm reception," said Wild coolly. "Tut, tut, man, keep your powder and shot for your enemies; I've come here at the risk of my life, to save yours."

"How am I to know that you are a friend;" inquired Johnson.

"I have come from Hicks," replied Wild.

"Where is he, has he escaped?" anxiously inquired the seaman.

"No;" replied Wild:" his goose is cooked, and so is your messmate's yonder, with about fifty pike-holes in his carcase."

"The devil seize him, his hastiness brought it all on himself by striking a young eriff who raised all this uproar, and I have lost the best pal a man ever had;" said Johnson mournfully. "But what's your name friend?"

"Jonathan Wild," he replied; "but we waste time here, follow me; I need not tell you to tread carefully, as you know the danger of this break neck road as well as I do."

"Don't fear for me," said Johnson, "take care of yourself; and raising the child in his arms, who, wearied by the excitement, had cried himself to sleep, they retraced their dangerous steps.

Lowering themselves on to a house some feet below the others, Wild opened a casement and entered a room. Descending the stairs, he conducted Johnson into a back yard, and unbolting a door, gave him directions, and a pass for leaving the Mint.

"Now hand me the brat," said Wild, "I daresay your'e glad to be rid of it; and mind, be silent about this night's business—mum's the word."

"Aye, aye," replied Johnson; and shaking hands with Wild, he quickly disappeared.

Ascending the stairs, Wild entered Mrs. Sheppard's room just as young Jack rushed in with the intelligence of

Jack Sheppard committing his First Robbery in a Gentleman's House where he was sent to Work.

the unfortunate predicament of Knee-bone. Depositing Francis on the bed, they sallied out to the rescue, as has been related in our last chapter.

CHAPTER VI.

SOME months had elapsed since the events we have been narrating in the preceding chapters had occurred, and Jack was now domiciled, as had been promised to his mother, in the house of Mr. Kneebone; much to the dissatisfaction of Mrs. K., who had from the first conceived a mortal dislike to our hero, and seldom missed an opportunity of expressing her displeasure at the arrangements: a course of proceeding on her part, which most married ladies un-

No. 6.

der similar circumstances can imagine, and which, no good behaviour of his (that is, if he had tried) could eradicate.

But as Jack was one of those scatter-brained, devil-may-care sort of fellows, who never trouble themselves about what people think of them, and possessed that kind of cock-a-hoop courage, which, like a hot mettled horse, is ever carrying its owner into some scrape or other, difficult to get out of, he was more likely to add to, than diminish the impression already formed of him by his mistress. And that he might not fail by his own unaided efforts perfectly to accomplish such a desirable state of things, he was kindly assisted to the best of their abilities, by the maid-servants, with whom he was no favorite, for, as he made it a point of leaving undone everything he was directed to do, and performing all manner of odd things that had better have been left undone, he contrived continually to keep them in hot water. Knowing how much he was detested by their mistress, and how gratifying to her was the relation of any little story to his detriment, they made him the scape-goat of their own transgressions, and took care to feed her with awful tales of his sins of omission and commission, which were afterwards retailed to her husband, whenever she wanted a subject of recrimination ; with such embellishments as her angry and fertile imagination could furnish ; and sundry digressions upon her patient submission to the ill usage she was subjected to, the indignity she suffered, by Mr. Kneebone's infamous conduct, in bringing his bastard into her house, her determination no longer to be insulted, with other flourishes of the like sort with which ladies are occasionally in the habit of treating their erring lords and masters at bed-time ; and which he, poor man, bore with that laudable resignation and meekness, which at that time is customary, merely tucking his head under the clothes to hear as little of the Jeremiade as possible, with many mental resolves of making up for his forbearance to his wife, by visiting the sins of the father upon the child, by giving Jack a glorious thrashing in the morning : which he usually received without flinching, and like one determined not to be the better for it.

In fact, Jack stood in the shoes of that unfortunate and much abused individual, nobody, who has all the mistakes, mishaps, &c., of a whole household laid to his charge, with this unlucky distinction, that Jack being somebody, all the punishment which nobody escaped fell to his share.

In short, there seemed to be an atrocious conspiracy formed against his peace and happiness, and, as to be continually the subject of the breath of slander, will tarnish even the purest virtue, it cannot be a matter of surprise, that under these circumstances, the unanimous voice of the whole establishment should declare, " there was not such an anointed young villain in London," and as that important domestic functionary the, cook, said, " if he dosn't come to the gallus nobody never ought."

As candid historians, we are bound to admit that the observation of that acute observer, the cook, was in some degree borne out by the fact, that from some peculiar idiosyncracy of character Jack never could be made clearly to understand the difference between meum and tuum, and had, but that we have no doubt proceeded from the nature of the education he had received, acquired some very extraordinary notions indeed of the rights of property, Though others go so far as to deny that it proceeded from any obliquity of mind or understanding, but arose solely from a marvellous glutinous quality which attended his fingers, to which, as to birdlime, every stray article closely adhered that he handled ; for which, his friend Blueskin who met him occasionally when out on errands had a cure in the shape of little pieces of copper or silver coin. But Jack was doomed in this as well as on future occasions to fall before the arts and wiles of woman : an unextinguishable feud had for some time existed between him and Mistress Janet, who strongly suspected him of trespassing on her manors, and as she did not tolerate any rival in levying blackmail on her mistress, she had determined to do her utmost to get rid of him the first opportunity. Besides, Jack had otherwise become obnoxious to her by his prying and inquisitive habits, by which he had become acquainted with sundry little secrets of hers in the sweethearting line, which for her own credit Mistress Janet would rather have remained solely within her own bosom, or at most confined to the knowledge of the parties more immediately concerned.

And now having pourtrayed the black spots in our hero's character, it is no more than common justice that we publish a redeeming trait, which was, the disinterested affection and kindness he constantly displayed towards the little orphan Francis Esdaile, the only being he seemed to love, and who returned Jack's kindness by standing up in his defence on all occasions, and as he had, from his gentle winning ways and affectionate disposition become an especial pet of Mrs. Kneebone's, he often had it in his power to return his friend's kindness.

"I'm blest if I cares," said Jack, one day when little Francis was endeavouring to comfort him after the infliction of some punishment he had provoked by an unlucky escapade, since which he had stowed himself away under the stairs to sulk, and had thereby lost his dinner.

"I'll run away Frank; I'm not a going to be huffed and scuffed about in this manner for nothing—See if I won't sarve 'em out for this, when I'm a man. I say, Franky, can't you crib us a bit of bread and butter, I'm so precious hungry."

"I won't steal, Jack; its wicked," replied Frank, "but I'll ask cook for some." "Oh, what's the use of that, she won't give it yer, if she knows its for me," said Jack.

Away however hastened Frank, and after a little coaxing, succeeded, and quickly returned to Jack in his hole.

"My eyes, that's prime," exclaimed Jack, "now mind what I say, Franky; when I'm a man, blest if I don't make 'em give up your fortin, whoever they is, if they's Dukes, or Lords," for Jack having settled it in his own mind that his friend was a Gentleman and unrighteously kept out of a vast property, had constituted himself the redresser of his wrongs.

"I know Mr. Wild knows summat about it" said Jack, "'cause I heard Blueskin and Mother a talking about you one day when they didn't think I heard it—but don't you recollect your father and mother, Franky?

"I can't recollect my father," replied Frank, "but I do my mother, I remember her dressed all in black, and, I shall never forget,"sobbed he, "her kind words, or her pale face, as she used to smile when she looked at me, or came to cry over me at night when I was in bed; but she's dead too. I remember the darkened room, and the black hangings, and the hearse and mourning coaches. And then a cross looking man, they said he was my uncle, took me and my sister away from home in a coach, and afterwards sent us to nurse Lee; and that is all I remember 'till I was brought away to London by a strange man."

Affairs were in this position when one day Jack, having escaped from the shop while his master was out and Mrs. Kneebone was at her toilet, cautiously ascended the stairs and entered the drawing room; after peeping suspiciously about, and returning to the door once or twice to listen that all was quiet, he began to rumage a casket Mrs. Kneebone had left open; and without any qualms of conscience proceeded to appropriate to his own use sundry trifles he found therein, such as a carved ivory bodkin case, a silver thimble and a pair of scissors. Having performed this notable exploit, he commenced a series of capers round the room, until espying a fine lace cap that had just come home from the milliners, he forthwith arrayed himself in it, daubing with his dirty fingers the delicate white satin ribbons with which it was decorated, grimacing in the glass the while; and then, with mincing steps mimicking the affected ways of mistress Janet, or the stately airs of Mrs. Kneebone. Having satisfied himself with this representation, he seized a sword of his master's, and throwing himself into a fencing attitude with a ludicrous attempt at fierceness in his countenance, he commenced enacting the part of a tragic hero, fencing and slashing about, and dooming at each thrust some one of his hated enemies to destruction, and fancying himself a mighty conquerer. In the midst of this amusement he suddenly heard footsteps on the staircase, and flinging down the cap and sword, he looked around for means of concealment.

"O criky, here's a go, shan't I ketch it," snivelled Jack at the thought of the hiding in store for him if caught in the drawing room. "I'm blow'd if I don't get in the clock-case." Into which he slipped, as quick as thought, just as the door opened, and Janet and Captain Hamilton entered.

No sooner had the gallant Captain entered the room, than suddenly turning round and closing the door, he clasped the pretty mistress Janet in his arms and, in despite of her struggles, ravished half a dozen kisses from her pouting lips.

"Have done, do! oh! here's somebody coming! be quiet!" exclaimed Janet, pretending alarm and offence at the liberty. "Look now! how you're tumbling my things; for shame!—la—I'll scream."

"Then I must take the precaution of stopping your mouth, Janet," said the Captain, repeating the offence.

"Well I'm sure, what next?" said Janet, smoothing down her dress and looking slantendicular in the glass; "what a man you are, I do declare you've spoilt my cap."

"Well then, my pretty Janet," said the Captain, drawing out his purse and taking her by the hand, while he insinuated the other arm round her waist, "here's something to buy another with. I'm so deeply in your debt for all your kind offices, I don't know how I shall repay you; but you look so good natured, and those cherry lips look so tempting, that I cannot refrain from stealing another."

"Thank'ee, sir," said Janet, curtseying demurely and looking at the bright guinea in her hand, when suddenly espying the new cap on the floor, she set up a screech. "O dear! O dear! that love of a cap quite spoilt; what will missus say—but I'll go up and tell her you're here, sir;" said she, casting a leer over her shoulder at the captain as she left the room.

Shortly after, Mrs. Kneebone having finished the adornment of her person, to which she had devoted unusual care, superadding a variety of embellishments and decorations, symbolical of her slaughterous designs on the captain, sailed into the room with all the confident nonchalance of a pretty woman conscious of the *impressment* of her appearance. Greeting the gay cavalier with a winning smile, she held out her hand, which he softly pressed within his own; and then carrying it with an impassioned air to his lips, he led her to a chair and seated himself beside her.

"Really, my dear madam," he exclaimed, in a rhapsody of admiration, "you are looking so enchantingly well, that I was under the impression it was some angelic vision that had descended from the realms above, and was about to throw myself at your feet to worship those divine charms."

To which, and other highflown compliments of the same nature, the lady replied with becoming spirit. But gradually their voices subsided into a low whisper, though from the earnest manner of the gentleman, and the flushing cheeks and humid eyes of the lady, it was evident that something of more than ordinary interest was the subject of their conversation.

In the mean while Jack, who had been exceedingly uncomfortable in the constrained attitude in which he had placed himself, endeavoured to obtain some relief by shifting his position, and in so doing dislodged a quantity of dust that had accumulated in the upper part of the clockcase, which so annoyingly titillated his olfactories that, after several attempts at suppression, a loud sneeze burst on the ears of the astonished pair.

"Gracious me! what's that?" exclaimed Mrs. Kneebone, in the utmost consternation—"What can it be?"

Glancing round the room, the captain, having satisfied himself there was nothing within to account for the phenomenon, laughingly suggested it must have been the cat; so encircling her slender waist with his arm, he gently drew the unresisting dame to his side, who, reclining her head upon his shoulder, permitted him to kiss off the tears that had started.

At this moment another suppressed sneeze was distinctly heard. A loud scream from Mrs. Kneebone was instantly answered by Janet (who had been listening at the keyhole of the door the whole time) bouncing into the room.

"For God's sake, what's the matter ma'm," cried Janet, as she flew to support her mistress, who was manifesting decided intentions to go off in a faint. By the aid of the smellingbottle, however, the lady had just recovered sufficiently to commence the relation of the horrid fright she had suffered, when a third sneeze from Jack shook the clock, and causing the chimes to jingle, betrayed the mystery.

Running to the clockcase, Janet opened the door and discovered our hero, who instantly digging his knuckles into his eyes, set up such a blubbering howl that completely drowned the exclamations of Janet, the laughter of Hamilton, and the lamentations of Mrs. Kneebone. Seizing him by the ear, Janet quickly dragged him out of his hidingplace.

"O the hideous little wretch," exclaimed Mrs. Kneebone, "he has been listening there all the time."

"How now, you young vagabond," said Hamilton sternly, "what were you doing there? Tell me instantly, or I'll cut your ears off."

"O please, sir," blubbered Jack, "I got in there to hide myself when you came in with Janet; and—"

"You little wretch," screamed Janet, fearful Jack was about to disclose that which she did not wish her mistress to hear, and bestowing on him a box of the ears that made the fire dance in his eyes. "I shouldn't wonder, ma'm, he's been at his thieving tricks, for I saw your casket open when I came in:" and forthwith diving her hands into his pockets, she dragged forth the stolen articles. "There, ma'am, I told you so," continued Janet; "and I'll tell your master directly he comes in."

"And so will I, what I see'd," retorted Jack; who, now having recovered his assurance, determined to turn the tables on his opponents.

"I shouldn't wonder, ma'm, he's been put in there as a spy, by you knows who," insinuated Janet: "but never mind—trust me for outwitting 'em. Come, sir, tramp—march; I'll spoil your spying. You'll tell your master, will ye—you sneaking little thief?" bestowing a cuff to drive him forwards, and then a shake to drag him backwards, till at last he was pushed out of the room.

A cabinet council was then held by the trio, as to what was best to be done in the emergency, to counteract the effect of the tale Jack would no doubt tell his master.

"Lor', ma'm, don't take on so," cried Janet. "If I was you I'd soon have the young spy out of the house—it's shameful. He must have been put up to it by somebody; but it's lucky we found these things upon him, which he stole out of your casket—they shall settle his business: and as for the rest, leave that to me—I'll find a way to set all things strait. Lor', ma'm," continued she, casting a sly look at Hamilton, "suppose I says it was me the captain kissed.

A course of operations having been decided on, by which it was determined to get young Jack out of the house, at all hazards—Hamilton, slipping another guinea into the hand of Janet, who, as she opened the streetdoor, contrived that the candle should be blown out— (though what passed in the dark we are unable to relate, further than the captain received a hearty slap on the back as he took his departure)—she tripped up stairs again to condole and concert with her mistress further schemes for the downfall of our hero.

Upon Kneebone's return, the storm burst on his unfortunate head. In a paroxysm of tears and reproaches, Mrs. Kneebone related to him the fright she had undergone, and desired him to take notice that the consequences might be more serious than he thought for. Then launching out into a full description of the atrocious robbery in which Jack had been detected, with a recapitulation of all his delinquinces from the first moment he crossed the threshold; in which she was corroborated by a running commentary, with notes, additions, and illustrations, by Janet, she concluded by declaring, that she considered her life in danger—that she was afraid to sleep in the house—that she was sure some of these days they should be all murdered in their beds— and that, unless Jack was instantly bundled out of doors, it was her determination that instant, to quit the house for ever, and fly for protection to her friends.

"I ll expose your hypocrisy; I'll proclaim your connexion with that shameless hussy, you base, tyrannical, hoaryheaded libertine : and then we shall see how you, with all your false pretences, will stand with the world. I'll show you what an injured wife can do—a faithful, unfortunate, ill-used woman."

Then flinging herself back in her chair, she commenced pumping up jets of hysterical sobs, accompanied by interjectional exclamations, of how barbarously she was treated; and calling Janet

to witness her fixed unalterable resolve of dying, rather than submitting to it any longer.

Goaded to distraction by their incessant clamour, which was poured forth with bewildering volubility, Jack—according to the usual method of administrating domestic justice—was summoned by his master to hear his sentence and receive the punishment awarded to him.

With great solemnity of manner, Kneebone proceeded to expatiate upon the idleness, insolence, dishonesty, and ingratitude our hero had been guilty of, in return for all the kindness and protection that had been bestowed on him ; and, after sundry moral reflections upon the consequences to be expected from such a line of conduct, and a highly coloured picture of the gallows here, and flames and everlasting torments hereafter, had been drawn in perspective for his especial behoof, he declared his intention of casting him off, and leaving him to the particular care of Belzebub, whose imp he was.

To all this pleasant and edifying discourse Jack paid but little attention, being intently engaged at the moment, with his thumb in his mouth, in counting the flies on the cieling. Janet, too, who had been an impatient listener to this rigmarole, here determined to have a fling at Jack, and said—

"Have you no shame in you, you obstinate pig? if I was missis, I'd have you sent to Bridewell, and flogged within an inch of your life, and that's too good for you, and the likes of you."

"I knows somebody else has a' got no shame," spitefully retorted Jack. "Didn't I see you a kissing the captain ?"

"O the base wretch!" exclaimed Janet, with a scornful toss of her head, and at the same time exchanging an expressive glance with her mistress, as much as to say, 'It's all right; you see how nicely everything turns out.'

"It's a perfect waste of time listening

to anything such an incorrigible little villain utters," angrily said Mrs. Kneebone; " there's no believing a word he says: he would not hesitate saying the same of me, I dare say."

" So I did," rejoined Jack savagely.

At this both the women turned up their eyes, and raised their hands as if horrorstruck at the audacity of the falsehood.

" And I see'd him kiss you behind the door," rejoined Jack, nodding to Janet, thinking to put a finishing touch to his charge.

" Well, saucebox," said Janet, " and if the captain did—I should like to know where's the harm?

" Janet!" exclaimed Mrs. Kneebone, in a tone of remonstrance, " I'm surprised to hear you talk in that improper manner."

" Lor, ma'am," returned Janet, " I'm sure I meant no harm ; I suppose one mus'nt speak to a man next."

By this time, Mrs. Kneebone judging that her husband was sufficiently led off the scent, desired to know, in an authoritative manner, if her desires were to be attended to, and whether she was to be considered the mistress of the house.

" You must, by this time, be convinced, sir, I should think, of what an ungrateful serpent you have been nourishing in your bosom," said Mrs. Kneebone.

Seizing Jack by the collar, Kneebone bestowed on him a cuff or two, and then proceeded to drag him out of the room, with the intention of chastising him below in the shop; when Jack, who seemed to have a decided distaste for the performance, after several ineffectual attempts to extricate himself from the grasp of his master, roared out,

" You'd better leave me alone, or you'll repent it, you stupid old cuckhold."

" What?" inquired Kneebone, letting go his hold, aghast at his impu-

dence; "old what? you insolent whelp!" at the same time lending him a kick a posteriori that projected him on to the landing-place; where Janet having planted herself, bestowed on him a slap and push that sent him head-foremost into the middle of the supper tray which the cook at that moment was bringing up stairs; and away both rolled to the bottom with a loud scream and louder crash. Springing to his feet, he seized a cold shoulder of mutton that met his grasp, and quickly disappearing behind a pile of woollen cloth, quietly sat himself down to enjoy the supper so unexpectedly thrown in his way.

Kneebone, half mad with anger and vexation, sallied out to Wych Street, to consult with his friend old Roger Wood, the carpenter; who, after listening to the relation of his domestic grievances, said—

" Well, neighbour, I see how it is, you'll never do any good with him at home, and as I am in want of an apprentice, I don't mind, to oblige you by taking the lad on liking. Send him to me if he's willing, and we'll see whether we can't make him a better man than his father; giving Kneebone a poke in the ribs, and at the same time giving vent to a laugh which sounded like the three expiring gasps of a throttled hen.

The preliminaries of the treaty being settled, to their mutual satisfaction, Kneebone hastened home to apprise Jack, who gladly assenting to the arrangement, quickly packed up his plunder, and to the joy of all parties, excepting little Francis, repaired to the house of his new master.

CHAPTER VII.

EARLY one morning Mr. Wild, who, having been actively engaged throughout the previous night, was in want of a little of the ready to carry on some of his plans, conceived a notable expedient of raising the wind.

As the government, at this time, were particularly anxious to gain information relative to the plans and partisans of the Pretender, and actively making inquiries after persons supposed to be connected with the cause, he determined to call on Mr. Kneebone, and in the first instance, by exciting his fears, to plunder him of as much as he could, and then proceed to sell the information he had already acquired.

On his arrival at the woollen drapers, he found only Mrs. Kneebone at home, who was employed alone, in imitation of Penelope, with her thread and worsted, mending a pair of blue stockings with red clocks; a circumstance which, perhaps, we might have omitted to mention, had it not served to show that there were still some ladies of that age who imitated the simplicity of the ancients.

Now Mr. Wild had on his first interview with Mrs. Kneebone, when disguised as a Jacobite priest, conceived that passion of affection, friendship, or desire, for that charming woman, which gentlemen of his age agree to call love; and considering this to be a favourable opportunity, commenced with many encomiums on her beauty, at which the lady seemed so much gratified, that a discourse thereupon ensued between them; which, if we could set down with great accuracy, would, we doubt not, be very edifying as well as entertaining; but, as we are in a prodigious hurry to proceed with the more important events of our history, our readers, we are sure, can easily suggest it to themselves.

At length the passions of Mr. Wild were inflamed by the wit and beauty of the lady to such a degree, that they transported him to freedoms so offensive to the impregnable virtue of Mrs. Kneebone, that though she had not learned the art of clenching her fist, proved nature had not left her defenceless, for at the ends of her fingers she wore arms and used them with such admirable dexterity, that the hot blood of Mr. Wild soon began to appear in several little spots in his face, and his full blown cheeks to resemble that part which modesty forbids a boy to expose any where but at a public school after some learned pedagogue, strong of arm, has exercised his talents thereupon.

Mortified at this unexpected rebuff, for Wild who had a very low opinion of the virtue of women, and a very high one of himself, had not anticipated such a reception, and conceiving that by his too hasty pursuit he had frustrated his intentions, like a prudent general began to cast about how to regain his lost ground, or, if necessary, effect a good retreat. With protestations, &c., of sorrow for his rudeness, laying all the blame on that resistless beauty which he said had deprived him of his senses, and arraigning his unfortunate want of command over himself, he humbly implored forgiveness with such apparent sincerity, that she—who was a woman, and not so much displeased but that she could forgive that of which she had been the cause—began to relent the severity of her treatment. Perceiving the advantage he had gained, he snatched a splendidly gold and pearl mounted miniature of herself, which had excited his cupidity—declaring he would part with it only with his life.

Now, as most females will forgive a liberty rather than a slight, it will be no matter of surprise that Wild was permitted to retain possession of it in earnest of his forgiveness: for, if a woman were to hang a man for stealing her picture, although it was set in gold, it would be a new case in law; but if he carried off the setting, and left the portrait, I would not be answerable for his safety, though Harmer were his attorney, Adolphus his pleader, and a Middlesex jury his peers.

And here our reader must pardon us if we stop to lament the capriciousness of nature in forming this charming part

Jack Sheppard spending the proceeds of his Robbery in the Mint.

of creation, designed to complete the happiness of man; with their soft innocence to allay his ferocity, with their sprightliness to soothe his cares, and with their constant friendship to relieve all the troubles and disappointments which can happen to him. Seeing then that these are the blessings chiefly sought after, and *generally found in every wife,* how must we lament that disposition in those lovely creatures which leads them to prefer in their favour those pithless individuals of the other sex, who do not seem intended by nature as so great a masterpiece; for surely, however useful dandies may be in the creation—and we are taught that not a louse is made in vain—yet these tailor-made popinjays, even that most splendid and honoured portion of

No. 7.

them, which in our island we love to distinguish in gold-laced scarlet coats and jingling jiggumbobs, are not, as some think, the noblest work of the creator. How melancholy then is the consideration, that any fine-dressed, glass-gazing, finical fop, especially if he be a Captain or a Colonel, shall weigh heavier in the scale of female affection than twenty Sir Isaac Newtons.

—" and yet it is
For such a civetted inglorious knave,
A jay, bedizened in the feathers of a peacock,
That many a fair and silly woman
Will leave the wing of a fine eagle spirit."

Now as we do not remember ever to have seen the true reason of this strange phenomenon accounted for, and as we scorn to keep any discovery secret from our readers, whose instruction as well as diversion we have greatly considered in this history, we shall here digress to communicate the knowledge we have acquired.

Know then, reader, that after much and severe study we have discovered the reason of this seeming whimsical preference for the inane glozing jargogle of superficial chattering jackanapes, and moth-like admiration of glitter, to the more solid yet less showy qualities of real worth, so universally exhibited by that beardless portion of creation whom the poet saith

'Nature made to temper man'
to be—.''

But here for the soul of us we cannot help suggesting for the benefit of future commentators, a new reading of this obscure passage. Surely man's hardhearted enough already! he don't want any tempering. It ought to be, whom

" Nature made to try the temper of man."

which we have no doubt will be considered an undeniable improvement in this slangwhanging age, where multiplicity of words passes for argument—noise for wisdom—and learning is supposed to consist in being able to call things by two or three names when one will do as well.

But this being a sub-digression, we will return to our digression.

Philosophers have observed, that by a wise ordination of Providence, all animated nature is formed with such organs and senses only, as are peculiarly adapted to their natural situation. So it is with women, whose minds being only constituted for the contemplation of little things, are naturally best pleased with trifles, gewgaws, and bawbles, and thus by an instinct of nature are led to prefer the society of fools — for whose especial enjoyment this world was undoubtedly made—to that of your musty philosophers and men of genius, who were created solely to be lighted up as tapers and consume

themselves for their especial enjoyment. But to proceed with our history, which we hope will produce much better lessons and more instruction than we can preach. Jonathan, who had thus with such infinite address, or impudence, or both, succeeded in mollifying the anger of Mrs. Kneebone, now, with admirable dexterity proceeded to turn his repulse into victory, for

——" women are pleased,
So that they're flattered, woo'd and teased ;
And well 'tis known that woman's mind,
Is still to noise and stir inclined ;
She would be marked and woo'd withal,
Rather to sin, than not at all,"

and are ready to pardon any extravagance in the men which appears to have been the uncontrollable effect of inordinate love.

Discovering that he was unable for the present to inspire the lady with love, he with that quick discernment of the advantage he had gained, which displayed his consummate knowledge of the windings, perplexing mazes, and weaknesses of the female heart, set about, by the most adroit flattery (which consists in acting the reverse of the physician, i. e. administering the strongest dose to the weakest patient) to fill to the brim the lady with love for herself, conscious that all that run over would fall to himself. And from his success, I think we may fairly assert that what was said by the Latin poet, of labour ; that it *conquers all things*, is much more true when applied to impudence.

By this artful conduct, having not only completely re-established himself in her good graces, but also raised himself considerably in her estimation, as a man of uncommon discernment, he prudently took his leave, with vehement yet respectful protestations of friendship on his lips, humility on his brow, yet the fiercest lust, resentment, and blackest revenge burning in his heart. Convinced that there were no hopes of accomplishing his designs upon Mrs.

Kneebone, while Hamilton was in the way, he determined on his instant removal.

Adjourning to a neighbouring tavern over a bottle of wine, he conceived a plan by which he thought he should be able, by one transcendental stroke of policy, at once to gratify his avarice, lust, and revenge. For Jonathan made it a rule never to do an injury to man or woman, by which he did not reap some advantage. Indeed he used to say, that by the contrary practice men often made a bad bargain with the devil, and did his work for nothing.

Having matured his scheme, he immediately resolved on putting it into execution, and dispatched a messenger to Kneebone desiring his immediate company on business of great moment. Upon his arrival, Wild took him by the hand, and with many expressions of friendship and concern informed him that, having heard from undoubted authority that Government had received information of the designs (which in fact he had supplied himself) of the Jacobites, and that they were in possession of a list of his partisans among which his name appeared, he had flown on the wings of friendship to warn him of his danger. Terrified at this intelligence, Kneebone earnestly implored him as a friend to advise with him how to act, to which Wild replied, that indeed he hardly knew but thought with money something might be done. " I know no surer means than bribery, Mr. Kneebone," added he, " and for a sum of money I have no doubt having some influence as you may suppose, that I shall be able to get you off." Kneebone eagerly besought him to stand his friend in this instance, assuring him of his ample means to reward any service he might render him.

" Well, well, Mr. Kneebone," said Wild, " if that's the case, make yourself easy, *I'm your friend*—but the sooner we set about it the better, as I have to see Mr. Wilcox, the King's messenger, to night so let me have £50 and you shall soon see what can be done."

Kneebone having quickly produced the required sum, which Wild forthwith conveyed to his own pockets, according to an excellent maxim of his, secure all you can," he continued " and now, Mr. Kneebone, I advise you, if you have any papers, to remove them, for most likely they'll search your house ; and I'll tell you what, to serve you, I'll take charge of them for you—they'll never suspect me."

Kneebone, with many expressions of gratitude, hastened home, and quickly returned with a small casket, which he entrusted into Mr. Wild's hands.

Having accomplished his first object, of getting some cash from Kneebone, and possession of these important documents, he proceeded to make him his tool for the accomplishment of his second—the removal of Hamilton ; for he was too cunning to appear as principal in driving away the cavalier-servente of Mrs. Kneebone—which, if known, he was conscious would not be the most likely way to effect his principal object—that of gaining her confidence ; so he had scheemed to throw the whole blame on her husband's jealousy, by which he anticipated reaping polygonal advantages, the opportunity of expressing his sympathy, and in aiding the escape of Hamilton, (for which he expected to be better paid than if he betrayed him)—to secure their mutual confidence, which was necessary to the ulterior proceedings he contemplated.

Thus doth your truly great man work by the hands of others, and keeps himself as much behind the curtain as possible ; for the stage of the world differs from that of Drury Lane or Covent Garden principally in this— that whereas on the latter the hero, or chief figure, is almost continually before your eyes, and the under actors are not seen above once an evening ; while, on the former, the hero, or great man, is always behind the curtain, and seldom or never appears, or doth anything in his own person. He doth, indeed, in this grand drama, rather perform the part of prompter, and instruct the well-dressed figures who are strutting in public on the stage, what to say and do. To say the truth, a puppet-show will illustrate our meaning better, where it is the master of the show (the great man) who dances and moves everything, whether it be the Emperor of Russia, or any other potentate, *alias* puppet, which we behold on the stage—but he himself wisely keeps out of sight; for, should he once appear, the whole motion would be at an end. Not that there is any one ignorant of his being there, or supposes that the puppets are not mere sticks of wood, and he himself the sole mover; but, as this (though every one knows it) doth not appear so visibly, *i. e.* to their eyes, no one is ashamed of consenting to be imposed upon—or helping on the drama, by calling the several sticks or puppets by the names which the master hath allotted to them, and by assigning to each the character which the great man is pleased they shall move in, or rather, in which he himself is pleased to move them.

We would suppose thee, gentle reader, to have very little experience in this world, to imagine thou hast never seen some of these puppet-shows, which are daily acted on the great stage; but though thou shouldst have resided all thy days in those remote parts which great men seldom visit, yet, if thou hast any penetration, thou must have had some occasion to admire both the solemnity of countenance in the actor, and the gravity in the spectator, while some of those farces are being carried on, which are acted almost daily in every village of the kingdom. He must have a very despicable opinion indeed, who can conceive them to be imposed on as often as they appear to be so.

The truth is, they are in the same situation as the readers of romance—who, though they know the whole to be one entire fiction, nevertheless agree to be deceived; and as these find amusement, so do the others find ease and convenience in this concurrence.

But to return to our history, which, having rested itself a little, is now ready to proceed on its journey.

After sitting some time sipping his wine in silence, Mr. Wild suddenly recommenced the conversation by complimenting Kneebone on the possession of so fine a woman for his wife.

"Why, man, you have a treasure there; and it behoves you to look sharp after it, too, for" said he with a knowing wink, "other people think so too: here's her health, Mr. Kneebone."

Having excited Kneebone's attention, whose smouldering jealousy wanted but a breath to fan it into a flame, he went on with many hums and ha's, and nods and winks, to inveigh, with much apparent acrimony, against the vices and profligacy of people of rank; which being a subject on which Kneebone loved to declaim, he turned up his eyes, and launched forth an awful tirade upon the wickedness of man, in which the little peccadilloes of his neighbour came in for their full share of virtuous condemnation: for your vicious men are ever great lovers of virtue that is in others, not in themselves. Having sufficiently bewailed the sinfulness of the flesh, Mr. Wild insensibly led back the conversation to the subject he desired—alluding by the way, to the many proofs he had given of his friendship for Kneebone, and the interest he took in his family and affairs—an interest which, he said, he was unable to account for.

"Now, Mr. Kneebone," said Wild, "I hope you won't think me impertinent in giving you advice on such a subject; but I've seen and heard with much concern a good deal lately of the goings on at your house: to be sure it's no business of mine, but, by G—, I'd not allow that swaggering coxcomb to be so much about a wife of mine."

Kneebone, whose suspicion of Hamilton had been aroused by many circumstances that had come to his knowledge, implored Wild to tell him what he had heard; and Wild, with much pretended hesitation, and some trifling additions, related what Jack had told him at various times. Kneebone, by these revelations, having been wound up to a pitch of fury, jumped up in his chair, and declared his intention of going home that instant, and turning his wife out of doors.

"Gently, man—take things quietly; suspicion's not proof. What, go and proclaim yourself a cuckold! why all the town will laugh at you. A bright thought has struck me, and if you'll be ruled by me, I'll show you a way by which you'll not only secure yourself with the government, but be revenged on this puppy as well. Kill two birds with one stone—that's my way."

Kneebone having expressed his willingness to be guided by Wild in anything, if it did not bring him in actual contact with Hamilton, of whom he had the utmost dread, Wild replied—

"I'll make that safe for you; now listen to me. Some of these Jacobite chaps, when they hear that government is up to their moves, will be ready to peach to save themselves—blow the gaff on you all. Now my plan is, be before hand with 'em; make your peace, and be revenged at the same time on this buck.

Kneebone, whose worser passions had all been excited during this conversation with Wild, was easily persuaded—first, by his cowardly fears for his own safety, and then his jealousy and hopes of revenge against Hamilton, —to turn traitor to his party: so over a fresh bottle they proceeded to arrange their future plan.

With such infinite address did this truly great man know how to play with the passions of men, to set them at variance with each other, and to work his own purposes out of those jealousies and apprehensions, which he was so wonderfully ready at creating, by means of those great arts which the vulgar call treachery, dissembling, and lying, but which are by great men summed up in the name of policy or politics, or rather pollitrics; an art, of which, as it is the highest excellence of human nature, perhaps *our* great man was the most eminent master.

Matters being thus arranged to their mutual satisfaction, and Kneebone somewhat re-assured by the positive assurances of Mr. Wild, the worthy pair proceeded to drink about with the utmost cheerfulness —drinking each others' healths, shaking hands, and professing the most perfect friendship for one another, till Wild, perceiving that Kneebone was getting fuddled, declared it was time to be off; so, with one hearty embrace, they separated —Kneebone determining to pay a visit to Dolly, and Mr. Wild, to make the most of the information he had obtained, proceeding to Mr. Walpole's, the Secretary of State, by whom he had been employed.

CHAPTER VIII.

SINCE his apprenticeship to Roger Wood, the carpenter, our hero had conducted himself with such exemplary propriety, and upon all occasions seemed to display so much liking for his business, that his master could not help congratulating himself on the acquisition of so industrious an apprentice, whom he loved to predict would soon become an excellent workman, and therefore sought by every indulgence in his power to render him comfortable.

Jack as he grew, evinced great hardihood of temper, and no inconsiderable quickness of intellect. In whatever he attempted his success was rapid; and a remarkable strength of limb and muscle seconded well the dictates of an ambition, turned, it must be confessed, rather to physical than mental exertion.

But suddenly a marked change came over his whole conduct. From being exceedingly quick and neat in his work, he became slow and careless; though still, when reproved by his master, who regretted to see so bright a promise marred, he was profuse in his declarations of amendment, and diligently exerted himself to make up for lost time.

But day by day his idleness and irregularities increased, whilst his fits of repentance and endeavours at reform became less frequent.

His Sundays, instead of being spent in attending church with his master and family, as hitherto had been his custom, were now either devoted to gambling with an idle set of blackguards, or in frequenting bull-baits, dog-fights, or other brutal exhibitions in the suburbs; until at length his misconduct became so notorious, that Wood, though a goodnatured, easy man, thought it absolutely necessary, since reproaches were of no avail, to try what a severe chastisement would effect.

Now, lest our readers should fall into that common error of those would-be wise-acres who are ever ready to consider misconduct in youth to arise from that innate love of vice which they say exists in the human heart—a canting phrase which has been invented by heartless, profligate parents and masters, who thus attempt to excuse their neglect of those moral duties in the education of youth, by charging upon Nature, that of which their own neglect is the cause—it will only be necessary to point out, that in the case of our hero, not only had it been his misfortune from the earliest period of childhood, to witness such scenes as none could look upon without contamination; for

" Vice is a monster of such hideous mien,
That to be hated needs but to be seen ;

But seen too oft—familiar with her face,
We lothe, endure, then pity and embrace."

But he had been marked as the prey of Jonathan Wild; who, having observed the shrewdness and boldness of the boy, had determined not to allow so promising a recruit for his gang to escape him.

Isolated, as it were, from all virtuous example; his associates only such as were serving an apprenticeship to vice; surrounded too by a polluted atmosphere, he was prepared to become the easy prey of the designing villain.

For the more effectually accomplishing his object, Blueskin was directed by his master in iniquity to lose no opportunity of enticing the boy from his work, to make him the partaker of his evil amusements, and initiate him into every description of profligacy.

In furtherance of this praiseworthy plan, and to encourage him in idleness and extravagance, Jack was supplied with occasional loans of pocket-money to enable him to support a figure among a numerous circle of young gentlemen, to whom he had been introduced, noted for their skill in living handsomely upon their own brains and the personals of other people, whose independent way of life, command of money, and amusing tales of the successful roguish tricks they had been engaged in, so fired his ardent imagination, that his utmost ambition was, that he might one day be able to emulate their exploits.

Thus idleness and vice were presented to his view accompanied with the most seductive pleasures, while industry and virtue were ever associated in his mind with irksome confinement and reproach; and the punishment so well intentioned by his master, instead of effecting the hoped for reformation, served but still more to confirm him in his evil ways.

" Wherever," says a living sage, "you see dignity, you may suppose there is expense to support it." So it was with Jack, who daily found increasing difficulties in maintaining his position among these juvenile chevaliers of industry.

Now the evil of all circles that are select, is high play; and Jack being somewhat embarrassed how to find the bustle to meet a debt of honour he had incurred, was tempted in an evil moment to appropriate to his own use a small account paid to him by a customer of his master's.

For several days the fear of discovery kept him in an agony of suspense. His flash acquaintance declined assisting him, and Blueskin to whom he applied, declared with many oaths that he was very seedy himself, and hadn't a coriander left; though at the time he had a bank note in his pocket which he had robbed a gentleman of in the playhouse passage.

At length, while at work at the house of a gentleman who was then abroad, and being in daily fear of his delinquency being detected, he was induced to plunge deeper into crime in the hopes of being able to replace the money he had embezzled from his master.

So surely does one false step lead to a second, or as the Persian poet has beautifully expressed it—"Our first fault, like the prolific poppy, produces seed innumerable; the winds waft them away, and we know not where they fall or where they may rise, but this we know, they meet us at every step upon the path of life, and strew it with plants of bitterness."

Having completed his job, he peeped cautiously about to see if the coast was clear, and then examined that and the adjoining rooms for any stray unconsidered trifle, not too hot or too heavy, that might be lying about.

Disappointed in his search, he muttered to himself, " Money I must have ; and I may as well die for a sheep as a lamb, so let's have a peep what's inside here." Approaching a bureau, he took

a tool from his basket and easily prised open the upper part. Thrusting his hand into each of the pigeon-holes, but in which there were nothing but papers, he hastily examined the small drawers under them, but to his grievous disappointment they contained nothing but some wafers, wax, a quantity of horsehair, fishing-lines, and the tackle of an angler. Laughing to himself, as his practised eye detected the secret cabinet, he pulled out two or three of the centre divisions of the pigeon-holes and exposed a small door—forcing back the lock of which, his eyes were gratified with the sight of the rich booty within.

" Blest if I aint in luck; here's a dollop of grannum!" he exclaimed; his eyes sparkling with pleasure as he weighed in his hand a purse containing a quantity of foreign gold coin. " Now let's see what the next dip in the lucky bag 'ull bring. S'elp me tater! a pair of Ridge specs! My eyes, here's buckles! Them's real dimons, I'll swear, they does so sparkle—that's the ticket."

Carefully refastening the door, he replaced the pieces of moveable wood that concealed it, and closing also the head of the bureau, with a bent nail, relocked it. Then opening with the same ease the drawers below, he discovered a quantity of silver-spoons, wrapped up among the linen with which the drawers were filled, and a handsome chased gold repeating watch with chains and seals attached.

Pocketting the watch, and stowing the spoons away in the bottom of his basket, he closed the drawers, and leaving everything apparently undisturbed, descended the stairs, and telling the servants he had finished his work, hastily left the house.

Fearful of discovery and pursuit—instead of returning home, he made his way in a contrary direction until he arrived at an unfrequented part of Montague Fields, where, seating himself on the ground, he feasted his eyes on his ill-gotten treasures.

Spreading out a quantity of doubloons on the grass, he rolled himself over and over them with frantic delight.

"Now I've rolled in gold, and that's more than many can say: strike me lucky, they must be five-pun pieces," said Jack, as he curiously inspected them. "What a bobbery there'll be when it's found out!"

Having sufficiently admired the diamonds in the buckles, which he held out in all manner of positions with the air of a connoisseur, and tried on the spectacles to assist his judgment, he returned them with a chuckle to their respective cases.

"Now this here rum gob-stick, and the sippers and feeders," he continued, as he returned a large gravy ladle and the other spoons to his basket, "I'll just hand over to Blueskin, he'll fence 'em with Jonathan as right as a trivit: and he'd better have these sparklers, and the specs too, I think. I'm blowed if he shal! have this pretty Clickman toad though —I'll keep that myself: shan't I cut a shine neither," he exclaimed with boyish glee, as he admiringly contemplated the handsome chain and seals, and then listened to the silvery tone of its bell as it repeated the hours and quarters.

Having arranged his plans in his own mind, he made his way through bye-lanes and courts towards home, but avoiding his master's house, he entered the White Lion, where he quickly espied the man he sought snugly ensconced behind a brestwork of pewter filled with the best october, with a cauliflower head. The slit across his frontispiece was embellished by the projection of a yard of clay, while round his whiskers and shaggy-matted head, curled the clouds of his ignited mundungus.

Swinging down his basket on the table with a self-satisfied air, he grabbed the pot, and nodding familiarly to Blueskin, took a hearty draught.

"Why, how now, young gallus! you improves, yer does. Wait till yer axed next time, will yer? or mayhap yer'll get a click in the gob. What brought yer here, eh? out of luck I suppose: it's no use coming the cadgering rig here."

Jack grinned knowingly at his companion, with a look which expressed as plain as if he had spoken it, 'You'll change your tune when you see what I've got.'

"What the devil ails yer, that yer stand there grinning like a Cheshire cat—can't yer speak?" angrily demanded Blueskin.

Jack forthwith related to him the piece of good luck, as he termed it, he had met with that morning; but carefully suppressing all mention of the purse and watch."

"Let's have a look at the swag, then," said Blueskin, "where is it?"

Jack nodded towards the basket, which Blueskin instantly opened, and rubbing his hands with delight, while a grin spread over his forbidding countenance, he exclaimed,

"Well, my promising bud, I allus said you'd turn out a right un; but are you sure nobody stagged you?"

Jack detailed the precautions he had taken to avoid a discovery.

"That's the ticket:—nor shown 'em to anybody?" inquired Blueskin.

"I should think not. I a'nt such a flat as that comes to, neither;" said Jack, indignant that his cunning or prudence should be questioned. "Catch me at that, indeed!"

We knows how to plant it safe," said Blueskin, "but if you'd a tried to sell such things as these, you'd a sure to ha' been done out of 'em, or else nosed on, you see, as your poor father was;—why, Jack, by the holy Moses, you're a precious sight cleverer fellow than he was, already, and no mistake."

"But yer hav'nt seen half yet," said Jack exultingly, as he displayed to the astonished and gratified eyes of Blueskin, the buckles and spectacles.

Jack Sheppard liberating Edgeworth Bess from St. Giles' Roundhouse.

"What do yer think of them?" enquired Jack.

"Real brilliants, by goles!" exclaimed Blueskin, grinning patronisingly upon Jack: "why, yer in the way to make yer fortin, my kiddy, if yer goes on as yer begins. I dosn't mind if we goes into pardnership; and to wet this here piece of luck, I don't mind standing Sam for a pot of humpty dumpty."

The humpty-dumpty quickly made its appearance; and Blueskin, with many imprecations upon his eyes, limbs, and circulating fluids, having drank all manner of luck and success to the future career of his protegé, then proceeded to amuse him by boasting of the various successful robberies he had

No. 8.

been engaged in during his course of villany.

"But the liquor's out, and it's time to top my boom," said Blueskin. "I must look arter Jonathan—and this here *wedge* must go into the pot; so you'd better toddle back to your shop, or the guv'nor will be kicking up a shindy: and we'll meet over at the Old Justice to-night to snack the bit."

"I'm not going back to old Wood's to-day," said Jack sullenly; "I'm off for a bit of a spree."

"Yer an't off for anything of the sort, you young dromedary," said Blueskin: "why, you fool, if there's any row about these things, you will be the first suspected if you're out of the way. I'll tell you what it is, Mister Jack, if you dosn't walk your chalks back in quick sticks, I'm damned if I has anything to do with the swag ; and then, maybe, yer'll be grinning through the bars by this time to morrow—and sarve you right too.   Come, come," continued he coaxingly, "you're only in pupil-straights yet, and yer must do as older and wiser heads directs you ; don't go to spoil what yer so cleverly begun. Now listen to me, Jack :—you've got a capital chance of doing business in your line, and you're a fool if you throws it away.   You must keep in with old Wood, and when you goes to work at a gen'elman's house, spy how the doors and windows are fastened ; and if yer keeps yer hearing cheats open, you'll maybe pick up from the servants where the plate is kept : so mind your game, and do as Jonathan and I tells yer ; and if you should get into trouble, we'll soon have you out."

Having delivered himself of this, for him, unusually long speech, and bestowed on Jack half a bull, which he with a contemptuous look chucked into his basket, Blueskin shoved the cases into his pocket ; and wrapping up the spoons in an old handkerchief, departed in quest of his pal : while Jack, shouldering his basket, returned to the carpenter's shop.

Flinging off his jacket, he made a pretence of commencing some work ; but after lazily planing the edge of a piece of wood, during which he grumblingly expressed his determination of giving old Wood the bag to hold the first opportunity, he commenced chanting—

"When Claude du Val was in Newgate
        thrown,
He carved his name on the dungeon stone ;
Quoth a dubsman, who gazed on the shat-
        tered wall,
' You have carved your epitaph, Claude du
        Val.'

        With your chisel so fine—tra la !"

"And now I think on it," murmured he, "I'm jiggered if I don't cut my name on the beam there.   What if Blueskin's words should come true—and I do make a noise in the world? how the people will come to see my name up there—perhaps a hundred years hence ! I'll do it : so here goes."

Placing a stool on the bench, and drawing a knife from his pocket, he commenced his work and continued his song.

"Du Val was hanged, and the next who came
On the selfsame wall inscribed his name :
' Aha !' quoth the dubsman with devilish
        glee,
' Tom Waters, your doom is the triple tree !'

        With your chisel so fine—tra la !"

"Crikey ! what a spooney I am to be sure !   I ought to have cut John instead of Jack.   Howsomever, it don't signify : nobody ever called me John as I knows on ; so I dare say I was christened Jack.

"Within that dungeon lay Captain Bew,
Rumbold, and Whitney—a jolly crew !
All carved their names on the stone, and all
Shared the fate of the brave Du Val !

        With their chisel so fine—tra la !"

"Save us !" ejaculated Jack ; "If this beam resembles the Newgate stone, I may chance, like the great man the song speaks of, to swing on the Tyburn tree for my pains.   No fear of that ; though, if my name should become as famous as their's, I shouldn't much care. The scarecrow of the hangman's three-cornered shop would never frighten me from taking to the road if I was so inclined.

"Full twenty highwaymen blithe and bold,
Rattled their chains in that dungeon old ;
Of all that number there 'scaped not one,
Who carved his name on the Newgate stone !

        With his chisel so fine—tra la !"

This S wants a little deepening though," said Jack, retouching the letter : "ay, that's better.   There !" he cried, jumping down and drawing back on the bench to examine his performance, "that'll do : Claude du Val himself couldn't have carved it better. I'm blowed if I an't a good mind to *cut my wood* in real earnest, and turn highwayman at once," said Jack, closing his knife.

"You have, have you?" thundered a voice behind him: "you'll cut wood and I'll cut flesh, then," said Wood, laying on about his dorsal region with his stick. "Come down, sirrah; I'll teach you to deface my walls in future. Come down, I say, or I'll make you, you vagabond—you idle, mischievous, young rascal!" So saying, Jack caught a crack on the shins, which soon brought him howling from the bench.

"And so you'll turn highwayman, will you, you lazy dog?" continued the carpenter, cuffing him soundly.

"Yes, I will," replied Jack sullenly, "if you beat me in that way."

Amazed at the boy's assurance, Wood left off boxing his ears for a moment, and looking at him stedfastly, said in a grave tone, "Jack, Jack, you'll certainly come to be hanged."

"I don't care if I do," said Jack doggedly. "But, be that as it may, I won't be struck for nothing."

"Nothing!" echoed Wood furiously. "Do you call neglecting your work nothing? singing flash songs, nothing? Is your recent idle discourse, and your present unblushing insolence nothing? Zounds! You idle, impertinent, incorrigible rascal! many a master would have taken you before a magistrate, and had you locked up in solitary confinement in Bridewell for the least of these offences. But I'll be more lenient, and content myself with merely chastising you.

"You may do as you please, master," interrupted Jack, thrusting his hand into his pocket as if in search of the knife, "but I would'nt advise you to lay hands on me again."

Mr. Wood glanced at the hardy offender, and not liking the expression of his countenance thought it advisable to postpone the execution of his threats to a more favourable opportunity; so by the way of gaining time he resolved to question him further.

"Where did you learn that song I heard just now?" he demanded in an authoritative tone.

"At the White Lion in our street;" replied Jack, without the least hesitation.

"A pretty house for an apprentice to frequent; why, you reprobate, it's the constant haunt of thieves. And who taught you that song—Jack Field, the landlord?"

"No," answered Jack, "a man named Blueskin. It was that song that put it into my head to cut my name on the beam."

"Pretty company for an apprentice to keep," replied Wood; "why the rascal you mention is a notorious housebreaker; he was tried at the last Old Bailey Sessions, and only escaped the gallows by impeaching his accomplices. Jonathan Wild bought him off. Be warned by your father's fate, and avoid bad company, and you may do well: you promise to become a first-rate workman; but you want steadiness—you want industry. Remember, Jack, idleness is the key of beggary, and if you don't conquer this disgraceful failing in time, you'll come to want. So now, Jack, get on with your work."

"So I will, master," replied Jack penitentially.

"Well, well, we shall see; good words without deeds are rushes and reeds." So saying, Wood left the shop.

For a few minutes after the departure of his master, Jack most assiduously stuck to his work, but gradually relaxing in his exertions, he at length threw down the saw and pulled out his ill-gotten treasures. The sight seemed to incapacitate him from all further labour; and first ascertaining that his master had gone out, he slipped on his coat and bolted from the shop.

Making his way to Monmouth Street,

he there exchanged one of the doubloons and rigged himself out in a pepper and salt suit and a scarlet waistcoat. He then proceeded to Montague Fields, where he cautiously buried the purse and the remainder of the money. But not so cautiously but that a Jew boy who had followed him for some time, endeavouring to sell him some oranges, and who from a distance had observed him look suspiciously about and then lie down on the grass for a while, immediately on his departure hastened to the spot and dug up his treasure.

After strolling about for some time, staring at every object he saw, and fancying every person who looked at him was an officer in search of him, and purchased for two shillings, at a bookstall, the life of Jack Hall and Du Val; he then rambled into the park, and laid himself down under the trees to read; but the humpty-dumpty overcoming his studious intentions, he shortly fell asleep.

We shall now transport our readers across the water to the Mint, and with their permission introduce them to the crowded company of both sexes which had congregated together in the parlour of the Old Justice.

This assemblage was for the most part, if not altogether, composed of those mercurial gentlemen who are afflicted with a morbid desire to pry into the mysteries of their neighbours' pockets; and to whom, consequently, vice in all its aspects was too familiar to present much novelty in whatever form it was exhibited.

Upon the centre table, which was strewed with pipes, rummers, and all the appliances of festivity, was placed a huge china bowl; one of those leviathan memorials of bygone wassailry, which we sometimes espy (reversed in token of its disuetude) perched on the top of an old japanned closet, but seldom or ever encounter in its proper position at the genial board. Perfume

subtle yet mellow, as of pine lime and arrack, exhaled from out the bowl, and mingled with the odour of the Indian weed, forming a delectable atmosphere. So, at least, seemed to think the bottle-nosed president; but who, by no means, confined himself to the gratification of a single sense, for the ambrosial contents of the china bowl apparently proved as delicious to his taste as its *bouquet* to the smell.

In a huge arm-chair, on a raised dais or platform, at the head of the table, loomed through the smoke, the demi-sacred, portly corpus of the master, Tobias; whose look of scowling importance, and drunken impudence, was designed to sustain his title, to call himself a blade of the huff: but who now, in his double capacity of president and publican, sedulously devoted himself to the due administration of the punch bowl. Not a rummer was allowed to stand empty for an instant. Toast, sentiment, and Anacreontic song succeeded each other at speedy intervals: his maxim being to make the most of the passing moment; the *dum vivimus vivamus* was never out of his mind— a precautionary measure, which is usually borne in mind by all gentlemen of precarious professions.

Close to his right hand was squatted Jonathan Wild; a devilish grin of satisfaction spreading over his truculent features as his bloodthirsty eyes gloated upon the scene. Near him sat Jack, evidently in the last stage of intoxication; his collar open, his dress deranged, a pipe in his mouth, and a half empty rummer before him. There he sat, receiving and returning, or rather attempting to return, for he was almost past consciousness—the blandishments of a young lady, who had her arm passed round his neck, whispering soft nonsense into his ear; while her eyes were intently gazing on the watch in her other hand, which she had coaxed Jack to give her. The name of this damsel was Elizabeth Lyon, better known as Edgeworth Bess; and as her fascinations will not, perhaps, be found to be without some influence upon the future fortunes of our hero, we think it worth while to describe her.

Bess could not be more than seventeen years old, though her person had all the maturity of twenty. In figure, she was fat and squabby, or what is termed Dutch built—with a round stem and stern. Her face was of the full-moon order, and a good deal freckled, with a nose that the French term *retrousee*, and the English, snubbed. Her eyes, which were small and blue, were surmounted by white eyelashes, while her carrotty locks dangled in unrestrained luxuriance down her back. She was habited in a loose bedgown robe of striped calico, slashed and embroidered *en gobble stitch* at the elbows; a two and sixpenny shawl was thrown with graceful negligence over one shoulder, though the other was a trifle too much exposed. Her headdress consisted of a bandalette of black velvet, in the centre of which, like a phylactery, shone a splendid mother-of pearl button; above which she wore a most valuable antique straw bonnet. Her delicate legs were encased in black worsted stockings, a la caraboo; and her feet were thrust into oriental slippers, which had curious contrivances for admitting the air at the toes.

On a chair opposite to Jack, whose rapid progress in depravity seemed to afford him the highest gratification, reclined Blueskin, perfectly at his ease—sacrificing to the god of flame, and encouraging Bess, by his looks, to ply him with the glass.

Nor was Jack the only stripling in the room. Not far from him was a knot of lads drinking, swearing, and playing at dice as eagerly and skilfully as any of the older hands.

Near to these hopeful youths sat an angling cove—*Anglice*, a receiver—bargaining with a buzman or pickpocket, for a suit, or to speak in more intelli-

gible language, a watch and seals, two cloaks—commonly called watchcases—and a wedge-lobb, otherwise known as a silver snuff-box. Next to the receiver was a gang of housebreakers laughing over their exploits, and planning fresh depredations: and at a private table were seated two dashing looking young gentlemen, of dissipated appearance, in long periwigs—habited in the riding-dresses of the period, and equipped in other respects for the road. Gay rings glittered on their fingers, and the remains of a roast fowl and bottle of Burgundy was before them.

"Come now, old Bacchus," shouted Hawkins, who having finished his supper, drew up alongside Tobias, and saluted him with a hearty slap on the back, "suppose you tip us a stave."

"A song, a song from the president, a song from the master—silence," roared all hands, making at the same time a prodigious clatter with their feet, hands and glasses.

"You do me too much honour gemmen," said Tobias, endeavouring to look modest, and emptying a tumbler of punch to hide his blushes. "I'm sure I shall be most happy. You must make all due allowance—hem." Clearing his throat, he trolled forth

THE TOPER'S PETITION.

O grant me, kind Bacchus,
The god of the vine,
Not a pipe nor a tun,
But an ocean of wine;
In a ship that's well mann'd
With such rare hearted fellows,
Who ne'er left the tavern
For a porterly ale-house.

Let the ship spring a leak,
To let in the tipple,
Without pump or long-boat,
To save ship or people;
So that each jolly lad
May always be bound,
Or to drink, or to drink,
Or to drink, or be drowned.

When death does prevail,
It is my design,

To be nobly entombed,
In a wave of good wine ;
So that living or dead,
Both body and spirit,
May float round the world
In an ocean of claret.

Loud acclamations rewarded the master's performance.

"I'll give you a sentiment, gemmen," said the master, when the hubbub had subsided a little ; whereat it instantly recommenced amidst loud cries of 'order—order.'

Rising on his legs, with one hand on the table to steady himself, while with the other he held up his glass, Tobias gave the following :

"Much sweeter than honey
Is other men's money."

An axiom which was received with all the enthusiasm which agreeable trueisms usually create.

"And now, Captain Hawkins," said Tobias, "we hav'nt heard your pipe to-night—there's never a cross cove of us all can throw off so prime a chaunt as yourself." After some little pursuasion Hawkins was prevailed upon to enliven the company, and warbled forth

THE FOUR CAUTIONS.

Pay attention to these cautions four,
And through life you will need little more.
Should you dole out your days to threescore,
Beware of a pistol before ;
                Before, before,
Beware of a pistol before !

And when backward his ears are inclined,
And his tail with his ham is confined,
Caution two you will bear in your mind ;
Beware of a prancer behind :
                Behind, behind !
Beware of a prancer behind !

Thirdly, when in the park you may ride,
On your best bit of blood, sir, astride,
Chatting gay to your old friend's young bride,
Beware of a coach at the side :
                At the side, at the side,
Beware of a coach at the side !

Lastly, whether in purple or grey,
Canter, ranter, grave, solemn, or gay,
Whate'er he may do or may say,
Beware of a priest every way :

                Every way, every way,
Beware of a priest every way !

"Bravo—bravissimo," chorussed the party.

"Fill up your glasses, my boys," said Hawkins, "and I'll give you a toast—

"Here's the health of that great donkey, the people ; and may we never want a saddle to ride them."

"Gemmen," said the master, rising and fetching the table a thundering rap with a small hammer by his side, " the next gemmen as I knocks down for a song, is a gemman whom we hav'nt had the pleasure of seeing amongst us for some time, having been on a visit of inspection to his majesty's dock yards, a gemmen as I means to say, as is game all up his back, an out and outer, a trump, and no gammon ; a cove as is down to every thing, and one for queering a greenhorn, easing a lushington of his yack, at bouncing or gammoning, has not his fellow. I calls on leary Joe, the fluefaker."

"Joe, my downy one, how are you?" "Here's luck to you, Joe,"—" Glad to see you among us again," cried a dozen voices, each proffering his glass to the object of his regard.

When the enthusiastic joy occasioned by this announcement had in some degree subsided, a short bandy legged man, with his hair arranged in Newgate drops, and a complexion like a red herring, arose. A Newmarket cut off coat adorned his back, in the outside pockets of which he sported two or three fogles of different colours ; a fancy waistcoat with pearl buttons enwrapped his carcase, black velvet knee kicksies adorned his thighs, and lace up mud rakers decorated his feet—a yellow neckscrag with a large fawny embracing it, completed his costume.

Nodding to the chairman and company, he said : " I'm werry much hobliged to yer all, gemmen, for your good wishes ; her", you see, once more, as right as a trivit, though they uses one werry scurvily where I comes from. The peck they guv us did'nt agree with my constitution, and ve poor kids was hobligated to vork like devils, from day break to sunset;" (loud cries of 'shame,' 'shame,' here burst from all parts of the room ;) " and then vorse nor all, no dab to dos on, but ve vos obligated to snooze in any place vot ve can: ve laid von a top o' t'other just like so many busters in a dead man's shop. But that's neither here nor there. I seed lots of old pals there, and they desired me to guv their respects to the guvnor, and all friends, ven I seed 'em. And as I've no more to patter about, I drinks all your good healths ; and vishes that every pris'n be seized with a sickness, and discharge the contents of its inside.''

When the hurrahs and bravos which greeted this eloquent narrative had ceased, Leary Joe, after sundry apologies, and as many sips at his glass, essayed to sing—

" As ve sailed down the river clear,
On the twenty-ninth of May,
Every ship as ve oame near
Ve heered the people say,
There goes a ship of rummy kids—"

Here Joe's feelings overcoming him, he declared his inability to proceed ; but, as the company declared their determination to take no excuse, he plucked up his courage, and dashed off with

The coves they calls me leary Joe ;
I'm known upon the mall,
I'm down, I'm up, I'm vide avake,
And nutty on each gal.
The beaks have often seen my mug,
And pigmen too a lot,
But still I sports my lily tile,
Likewise my fancy mot.
Tickle'em tol fol iddity ol rifum tooral hey.

My father vos a cracksman good,
And lots o' booty bagged,
Until his brother peached on him,
So he, poor kid, got lagged ;
But still he got no good by that,
As you, my coves, shall hear,

For prigging a fogle he got lagged,
For seven long year.
Tickle'em, &c.

Then I vos left a orphan,
As you may plainly see,
But soon to follow my old man's steps
I'd a propensi-tee ;
So I fingered all vot I could catch,
But vos seldom cotched myself,
And many a rich swag I laid up
Upon the fencing shelf.
Tickle'em, &c.

Then here's success to leary coves,
Those absent and those here,
And may all of 'em have pluck enough,
A sarcy pig to scare ;
Success to those who're in the start,
Likewise to them vots out,
And may the clumsy clinkers,
Set light their shins about.
Tickle'em, &c.

Long life to every fancy chap
A tramping ou the town,
And may they never want a hog,
A cooter or a crown ;
Long life to those vots gone abroad,
Upon the briny sea,
Good luck attend each leary cove,
Wherever he may be.
Tickle'em, &c.

" That's all, genelmen," sung Joe in the same voice, continuously with the last words of his ditty, so as to lead his hearers to suppose it was part of the song ; and at the same time giving the table a tremendous rap, he said, " I ought to be velted for not singing better:" with which apologetic depreciation of his harmonic powers, he flung himself back in his chair, and recommenced smoking furiously.

Your health and song, Joe," said the master; " what shall we say after this excellent chaunt ?"

" Vy, this is vot I've got to say," rejoined Joe ; " confusion to all pigmen, peachmen, and beaksmen !"

Again the pots, glasses, hands and feet, were put into requisition to express the hearty concurrence of the hearers in the sentiment, and which was only put a stop to by the master rising and soliciting their polite attention.

"Genelmen of the Mint," said Tobias.

"Hear, hear!—Order!—Silence!—Cut it short old feller!" and cries of go on, greeted the orator from all parts of the room.

"Genelmen, when I first succeeded to the high office I now hold, there were three other shops t'other side of the water, where the oppressed and persecuted debtor was safe from the hell-hounds of the law."

"Aye, aye—so there was," answered several voices.

"Well, my loyals," pursued the master, "upon the occasion of my accession, Alsatia, Salisbury, Savoy and ourselves, met in congress here, in our palace of justice, to consult upon the best means to be pursued for upholding our rights, privileges, and 'munities against the encroachments of the pirates of St. James's. And a roaring night—one worthy such mighty monarchs—we had of it, I can tell you. We quaffed our punch, and smoked our pipes right royally. A length, Alsatia turns to me with a sigh, and says, 'Mint!' says he, 'you're in comfortable quarters here, my Trojan.' 'Why, tol-lol for the matters of that,' says I—'I don't complain; and you an't so worser off neither at the Friars.' 'Ah!' says he, with a melancholy shake of his head, 'I'm thinking we never shall see such times again as is gone; I'm afraid we're in queer street.' 'What do you mean?' says I, taken quite aback. 'Why, I hears,' says Alsatia, 'there's a conspiracy going on to take away our charter.' 'Gammon,' says I, 'tell that to the marines. They can't—its unconstitutional; why, the bishops wouldn't stand that. That cock won't fight, Ally—I an't so green as all that. Why, yer might as well tell me they're going to take away the city-charter, and cabbage the Lord Mayor.' 'It's no gammon,' says Savoy, 'I knows it's too true—for I has it from the best authority. Lord O. M'All, who is on a visit at my court, told me confidentially yesterday, that they're a going to pass an act of Parliament to make every body pay their debts.' 'We'll become the prey of the Philistines,' groaned Salisbury. 'I should like to know how we're to live in such a state of things? 'Why, rot me!' said I, thumping the table till the glasses jingled again, 'if I'd submit to it; let 'em try it on here—I'd pretty soon spoil their plans, I warrant. 'How?' asked all three. Why, hang every bailiff as dares set his dirty foot in my territories,' says I; that 'ud put a stop to 'em. 'Damn it! we'll do it!' says they, filling their glasses and looking as ferocious and sanguinary as three Saracens; 'here's your health, Mint.' But for all they talked so bounceably, they were afraid to do it; and what was the consequence? Where are they?"

"Hear, hear! Ah! where are they? Vy, up the flue!" echoed the company.

"Genelmen, they're gone to pot; and sarve 'em right, the cowardly curs!" continued the master. "If they'd had the pluck to have scragged the ban dogs as I proposed, why the bailiffs couldn't have scragged them. Now, when they tried it on with us with that unlawful act, passed in the reign of the usurper Orange Billy: (and I should like to know how a foreigner, and a Dutchman, is to know anything of our blessed constitution. If the rightful king had been on the throne, that unconstitutional act would never have received his assent: the Stuarts, God bless 'em, always sided with the debtors.)"

"Hear, hear!" vociferated the Minters.

"What did we do? why I means to say, as shouldn't say it, by our brave resistance we not only firmly established our rights and privileges, but covered ourselves with glory. Let 'em try it again if they dare."

"Hear, hear! Bravo Toby—you're a trump!" shouted several voices.

Jack Sheppard's escape from St. Giles's Round House.

"And I should like to know, continued Tobias, "what were the grounds of this outrageous attack on our rights. They call us rogues and vagabonds, and themselves honest men. A fico for their honesty. Why what more do we than is done every day by the lawyers, parsons, soldiers or ministers of state?

"And where is the mighty difference between us and these honest gentry?

"Does it not require the same genius to compose a prig as a sta'esman? Is not a guinea as valuable in a leathern as an embroidered purse? As a cod's-head is a cod's-head still, whether in a pewter or silver dish, would not the same capacity which qualifies a mill-ken, a bridle-cull, or a buttock and file, to any degree of eminence in his profession, likewise raise a man to the highest offices in the state."

"Now, my Nabs, I'll tell you, the

No. 9.

difference is simply in a choice of words. They call their own actions by different names, to what they do ours. They are never rogues so long as they call themselves honest, or commit a crime so long as they can call it a virtue."

"With them oppression is order; extortion, church establishment, and taxes is blessed constitution. That which they would call indomitable courage in themselves, they term bullying in us. What in their great men they laud as admirable address, would in one of ours be designated as wheedling; in short the same actions which in themselves are virtuous, are in us vicious—and we forsooth must pay the penalty."

"But this state of things won't last for ever. I prophecy the day will come, when not Southwark alone shall be the place of refuge for the unfortunate (for our principles and practices will spread in despite of the persecution we experience and their endeavours to destroy us) but all London, nay even all England itself, shall become one mint."

"When the snaffling lay shall be considered a pleasant pastime; the nubbing cheat thrown down, the sherriffs ball be abolished, and the craping curl and quod culls on the pension list, when Newgate, Ludgate, and the Gatehouse are razed to the ground, and Bridewell and Clerkenwell destroyed, when it shall no longer be in the power of one man to seize on the person of another because he owes two pounds, and confine him in prison, away from his family, 'till he owes fifty; when the Never-wag man of war is cut adrift, and the King's Bench broken down. But as I shall have the ground-sweat long before that day comes, we'll make the most of the present. Take care of yourselves, my cross cronies and your sovereign will take care of you. But before I set down I have to propose a toast which

I am sure will be received as it deserves, with enthusiasm. It is the health of a stranger who has this evening become free of the province—of Mr. John Sheppard. His dad was an old customer of mine, and I'm glad to see his son treading in his steps—he couldn't be in better hands than those in which he has placed himself.—Mr. Sheppard's good health and success to him."

The master's toast having been received with a deafening round of applause, he sat down amid the cheers and clatter of mugs and glasses. Upon which Jack having with some difficulty raised himself to a perpendicular, blew his nose, stroked down his hair, and pulled up the slack of his breeches, essayed to return thanks; but the room at that moment unfortunately giving a lurch: our hero pitched forward among the glasses and bowls on the table, and thus deprived us of the pleasure of reporting his speech, from whence after some kicking and scuffling, he was conveyed to an adjoining bench to sleep off the effects of the punch, while the false and fickle Bess departed to her libken, in the society of Leary Joe.

———

CHAPTER. IX.

OUR strict regard to veracity in this veritable history, renders it impossible to indulge our reader's curiosity with a full and exact relation of all the actions in which our hero was engaged during the course of his education for the bar. For as there are such various and contradictory accounts of each of his exploits, *one* of which only can be true, and possibly and probably *none*, to which latter opinion we incline, instead of following the vulgar general method of historians, who in such cases set down the various reports, and leave to your own conjecture which you shall chose, we shall pass them all over: merely premising the whole time was one continued scene of whoring, drinking, thieving and removing from one place to another; very necessary to the full development of our hero's powers, but not worthy of our reader's notice; but though this is a very short chapter it contains infinitly more time, and less matter than any other in the whole story.

To confess a truth, we were so ashamed of the shortness of this chapter, that we would have done a violence to our history, and inserted an adventure or two of somebody else, and for this purpose have delayed the publication of this number a whole week in the hopes of being able to filch something suitable to our purpose from that Gradus ad Patibulum, "the Chronicles of Newgate;" but to our great sorrow we could not extract a single incident worthy of our hero, that would justify the theft to our conscience.

When we consider the ridiculous figure this chapter must make, being the history of no less than three years, our only comfort is, that the history of some men's lives, and perhaps of some men who have made a noise in the world, are in reality as absolute blanks as those of our hero. As therefore we shall make sufficient amends in the sequel for this inanity, we shall hasten on to matters of true importance and immense greatness.

CHAPTER. X.

"Past nine!" exclaimed Blueskin in an impatient tone, as he stood at the door of the White Lion, listening to the chimes of St. Clement's performing their stumbling, jangling burlesque of the 104th Psalm, which has about as much resemblance to the sacred melody, as though a collection of bells, blacksmiths' anvils, tin pots and paving stones, were to get moppy at a party in the steeple, and tumble down a flight of stairs. "What the devil's become of the lad, and such a fine night too."

The night in question, which called forth this eulogium, was indeed a very fine night of the sort. A London particular fog, as dark as if all the niggers in Africa had been stewed down into atmospheric soup enveloped the city as with a pall, and totally obscured the miserable twinklings of the street lamps, which at that day, (or night we should say,) even at the best of time, served but to make darkness visible.

Just as his patience was becoming exhausted, a voice was heard from out the palpable obscure, singing:—

"The Mob too has ris'n
And let out of pris'n."

With the jailor's own keys, (but 'tis no fault of his'n,)
Some hundreds of millkens, and fences, and prigs,
Who are playing all sorts of queer antics and rigs."

"Now Scapegallows," interrupted Blueskin, as the party approached him, "you're keeping up the ball, I don't think; what's the order of the day?"

"Ah, my smashing cove," replied Jack, as he stepped up to him, "I'm going to visit St. Giles'."

"Going to visit the devil; stow yer whid and come along with me; I've been looking for yer these two hours, here's a night for business."

"No I won't," replied Jack, sullenly.

"Why, whats up now?" enquired Blueskin, in astonishment at Jack's sorrowful look "damn it man, your face is as long as a mare's baby."

"Why Bess has been grabbed, and is boxed up in St. Giles' for taking a fawney from a lushington."

"Ha! ha! ha!" laughed Blueskin, at the idea of Jack's concern. "Don't be downhearted; it an't the first time Bess has passed the night there—she won't take cold; and we'll make it all right in the morning. Come, come, there's some right 'un's inside."

"Who's there?" inquired Jack.

"Why, Bill Field, Tim Dun, and Hell and Fury: we've been waiting for you; and we mean to try old Kneebone's crib to-night."

"Well, then, they must wait," rejoined Jack doggedly: "I'll go nowhere till I have my little ladybird out of the roundyken: after that, I'm your sort for anything; though I don't half like those pals of your's."

"Hollo! what's in the wind now?" inquired Blueskin; "you're as full of likes and dislikes as a snivelling wench."

"Why, what's the use of such a damned coward as Field," replied Jack; "he's fast enough after his reg'lars, but the first to sherry if there's any danger: and as for Jim, you know —"

"Hush!" whispered Blueskin; "you don't know him; Hell and Fury is a good 'un at bottom."

"Well, I'm off," said Jack resolutely.

"Stay a moment, while I get my sticks, Jack," cried Blueskin, as he entered the While Lion; from whence he quickly returned with a brace of pistols, which having stuffed into his pockets, he exclaimed,

"Now, here's go with you; I'll stand by you, my boy, whatever comes of it."

Without vouchsafing a reply, Jack moved quickly on up Wych Street and Drury Lane, followed by his former master, but now companion in vice.

During the time that has elapsed since our hero's introduction to the Mint, a manifest improvement had taken place in his outward form: from a slim ungainly youth, he had sprung up into a tall athletic man, though the down was still on his cheek. But the improvement was only external. Internally, the change was for the worse; and the effects of the evil company he had kept, combined with the constant gratification of the worst passions of

the heart, was strongly marked on his face—so often the index of the mind; and which displayed that character of dogged resolution and obstinate perseverence for which he afterwards became so notorious.

Passing quickly along Broad Street, but which was then narrowed by several blocks of almshouses, which stood in the middle of the street—they entered Kendrick Yard, a dirty unpaved mews, filled with dilapidated, half-roofless stabling; superannuated hackney coaches; and the debris of various antique wheel machines.

The inequalities of the ground were filled with a compound odoriferous fluid, consisting of the drainings from the dung-heaps, and the blood and garbage from one of the buildings occupied as a slaughterhouse.

At one end of the yard stood a tall, detached, circular stone-building, resembling a martello tower, and surmounted with a huge key by way of weathercock. This building was St. Giles' roundhouse; an erection evidently of some antiquity; and from its echarped loopholes, and general appearance of strength, was no doubt originally a place of refuge and defence, in the turbulent periods of our early history.

The small windows were strongly barred; and the entrance, which was a considerable height from the ground, and approached by a flight of ruinous steps, was defended by a strong oaken hatch-door, studded with iron nails—the lower half of which was furnished with long spikes; and in the upper appeared a small grating, for the purpose of reconnoitring.

As they approached the building, Blueskin inquired of Jack, who hitherto had maintained a sullen silence, what he intended to do.

"Just you keep a sharp look out," said Jack; "and if anybody comes, give us the office—leave the rest to me; there's nobody here but old Brown and his wife on a Sunday night."

So saying, he marched boldly up to the door, and knocked authoritatively with his stick.

"Now, then, St. Giles," said Jack, "am I to be kept here all night? Come, stir your stumps."

"Coming, coming," said the beadle, as he shuffled towards the door.

"So is midnight," retorted Jack.

The slide was withdrawn, and after a long survey, Brown demanded in an important tone what he wanted.

"Why, I want to come in," replied Jack.

"None is admitted here but parochial officers," said the beadle with dignity.

"Come, come, Mr. Brown," said Jack, "if you don't mean to let me in, I must go back to Mr. Wild."

"Mr. Wild!" exclaimed the beadle; "Why didn't you say before you came from Mr. Wild?" and, after taking a second and more particular view, he forthwith proceeded to unlock and draw back the ponderous bolts to admit his visitor.

The room into which Jack stepped was of considerable size, and furnished with a stout table and a huge leathern-hooded chair, in which reposed, when on duty, his high mightiness the night-constable; and in front of which was a strong bar, to keep off unruly prisoners. Around the sides of the room, were fixed benches for the repose of the supernumerary charlies; and against the walls hung an assortment of staves, brown bills, (weapons then borne by the watch), musquets, handcuffs, great coats, and lanterns.

"Now, sir," said Brown, when he had carefully refastened the door, "I've got you safe enough. Ha! ha! ha! Mr. Sheppard; you thought I didn't know you, eh? you've nicely walked into the trap. 'I want to come in!' Ha! ha! How do you like your quarters?"

"Give me your keys, and don't stand jabbering there, you old fool!" said Jack, with a determined aspect.

"Ha, ha; very good, Mr. Sheppard; we'll show you the way to a nice apartment," said he in a jeering tone, laying his hand on the collar of Jack.

"Don't make a fool of yourself, Mr. Brown," replied Jack; "the prison's not built that can keep me."

"We'll see, we'll see, young hempseed," replied Brown; "if you get out of here, I'll forgive you: now, come along, young gentleman."

Suddenly bringing his leg behind him, and driving his elbow into his face, Jack easily floored the beadle; and while he laid sprawling on his back, placing his knee on his paunch, quietly proceeded to divest him of his keys.

At this moment the beadle's wife rushed to the rescue. Seizing Jack by the hair, she dragged him backwards off her spouse, at the same time bestowing on him sundry well-intentioned cuffs of the chops. This diversion enabled Brown to regain his feet, and possess himself of a huge staff, with which he dealt our hero so tremendous a whack on the sconce just at the moment he had extricated himself from the embraces of the lady by ungallantly tumbling her on the ground, that he was compelled unceremoniously to seat himself on her feather-bed form, with such an impulse, as to produce a distinct double report.

Quickly recovering himself, he closed with the beadle; and, wresting the staff from him, favoured him with a bonnetter that sent him sprawling into the corner, from whence he prudently abstained from rising—contenting himself with shouting murder, and calling upon his wife for assistance. But she, good lady, not having yet sufficiently recovered her wind, was lying helplessly on her beam-ends, puffing and blowing like a grampus.

Having disabled his opponent from further interference, he methodically proceeded to unlock the cell that confined his doxy.

"Bear a hand, Bet; now's your time

old gal: you see I an't forgot my promise."

To which invitation the lady replied by dancing out of her den into the middle of the room; clapping her hands with joy, and singing defiance.

"Oh, there you are!" screamed she, planting her arms akimbo, as she spied the watchhouse-keeper bleeding on the ground.

"Did yer think to grab my little Jack, you nasty, stinking, ugly, squinting old varmint?" screamed Bett. "I say, Jack, vouldn't he make a nice figure-head for a night-cart?"

"Come on, Bet," said Jack, "never mind him; he's got as good as he brought: but let's see what he's got in his pockets."

In the mean while, Mrs. Brown had silently rolled her bulky carcase on end, and arming herself with the fire-shovel, made a slashing cut at Jack, in the hopes of disabling him; but which kind intention was frustrated by Bet, who, spying the manœuvre, seized her by her dishevelled hair, exclaiming—

"Don't flurry your milk, old lady;" at the same time lending her half a dozen hearty dowses in her potatoe trap, and finishing by scientifically bundling her under the grate.

"That's your sort, Bet," said Jack admiringly.

At this moment the signal of some one approaching was made by Blue-skin. Unlocking the outer door, he exclaimed—

"Nammus, Bet—nammus, quick; the beaksmen are on the nose. I say, old bottle-nose, next time I come I hope you'll give me a better reception: you promised to forgive me, you know—eh? take a carrot, old boy."

Then politely wishing them good night, he locked the door on the outside, and shying the keys over the roof of one of the stables, hastened, laughing, after his companions.

———

CHAPTER. XI.

THE preceding chapters have depicted the boyhood, and education of our hero. In our last we have seen an exploit that must procure him an indisputed renown for galantry and daring, however charmless his dulcinea, or unchivalresque the St. Giles' Round House, and its guardian may appear in the eyes of the romantic reader. But the petty rogueries of childhood, and the gallantries of youth, must now yield to depredations more serious in their nature, and more ruinous in their consequences to his character. Sheppard has entered on his career. The propensities of his nature, strengthened by indulgence, became habits before reason had assigned sufficient strength to issue its veto, and their unhappy slave was thenceforward to pursue with impetuosity, a course that astonished the most reckless and callous spirits. Many are the incidents we might recount—many the scenes we might describe, for the amusement of the reader, did not our limits compel us to pass them over in silence in order to give a due prominence to what really form important features in the life of this notorious housebreaker. Still we must caution those who may honour these pages with perusal against supposing that such events form the whole instead of the striking points of our hero's history. We must invite his imagination to fill up the void we are obliged to leave. We must remember that with Jack Sheppard theft was not a desperate expedient to secure him from the misery of starvation,—the refuge of an indolent man, incapable of the application employed by his fellows to secure a livelihood; or a shorter road to wealth, pointed out by the cravings of avarice; but a career, a profession, a *passion*. We do not therefore find his life occasionally marked by a daring exploit the result of necessity, or temptation, but it presents us with an even tissue, in which knavery, obstinacy, and boldness are the chief materials of the web. We may well suppose that in a mind like Sheppard's the review of each day's adventure was but the prelude of deeper scheming for the morrow, the success or failure of the present alike inspiring courage for the future. It is difficult to conceive the excitement of such a mind, the vigour of its hope, firmness of its purpose, its triumph in success; still more difficult to paint the scenes in which it played a conspicuous part—deeds of secrecy with their adjuncts, gloomy nights, dark lanterns, suppressed breaths, strained eyes, and muffled footsteps,—midnight orgies, where burning liquor, and burning kisses, wine and women contend for the mastery;—or flight and concealment with their privations, suspense, hunger, cold, and capture.

Jack was fully acquainted with the change of his new calling, and admirably qualified to go through them. He had already plundered extensively, revelled gloriously, and escaped justice with rare good fortune; when a closer acquaintance with the latter inflexible lady awaited him.

It is only by a long process that the mind of man becomes thoroughly bad. The heart may incline fondly to base propensities, yet will there be a sun glimpse in the storm—signs of the nobility of human nature, breaking through habitual degradation. Jack Sheppard, the housebreaker could stretch forth his hand with friendliness to an associate, and while he outwitted the emissaries of the law, became the dupe of his boon companions.

It was high noon; Sheppard loitered through his own regions, the dense neighbourhood of the Seven Dials. His step was slow, his attitude slouching. The housebreaker's vigour and energy could not be traced in the listless appearance of a debauchee recovering from the revels of the past night.

It had been a glorious night with Jack. Premises long eyed with envy as much for their difficulty of access, as for the treasure they contained, had yielded to his practised hand, and untiring perseverance. The night proved unfavourable, but there was no resisting—the desire—the thirst for plunder. In vain Bess urged the brilliance of the moonlight, Jack pointed to the only cloud in the heavens.

"It is my friend," said he "and will douse even that glim."

As he spoke, he drank off the dram Bess had filled, buttoned his coat around him, seized his instruments, and entrusted the dark lantern to his pal.

How dead was the silence of the narrow street they entered; how deep the gloom through which they glided; for the moon beams could not penetrate the lofty avenue of houses; and gas, in our days a faithful adjunct pressed into the service of morality, did not then exist.

"Hush!" whispered the voice of the woman, for Bess then abandoned as she was, had a partiality for Jack, which gave her the exquisite vigilance peculiar to the anxiety of woman—"A footstep."

They stood aside beneath a doorway, and a man passed them. Jack recognized an acquaintance for whose aid he had however no particular demand, and he allowed him to pass without notice. Sheppard had not, however, escaped the man's glance; but thieves are punctilious, and neither spoke. A few minutes brought them to the scene of the meditated robbery. The difficulties were apparently insuperable; but were met by the perseverance to which all things yield. An entrance was effected, a rich booty carried off. To Bess was awarded an article of apparel of more finery than value, and a glorious carouse followed that but for the stupor of intoxication and day-light would not have ended.

But where is the hero, whose achievements are not followed by lassitude, especially when his prowess contends with the strength of the bottle? Vanquished by that charming antagonist over-night, Jack, as we have seen, bore every symptom of his complete overthrow at mid-noon on the ensuing day. They are dreary things the blue-devils, and especially are they dreary to a buoyant spirit, such as Sheppard's: it was therefore with no little pleasure that he met with an old friend, the proteus of thieves, James Sykes, and renowned for the saintly cognomen of Hell and Fury.

On this occasion, the latter gentleman displayed an unusual cordiality towards our hero; and the *great sharper* was yet green enough to suffer the cordiality of his friends to touch the kindliest strings of his own heart. The tankard soon foamed before them; as infallible a restorative for a drooping rake, in the opinion of Jack Sheppard, as improving science has since pronounced Seidlitz water; and their deep libations proved each party the most friendly of friends. The active spirit of our hero, however, soon seeking a change of diversion, a game of skittles was proposed; and the friendship displayed over the tankard was still further exhibited in the skittle-ground.

"Take care, Hell and Fury—I shall blab," said Jack, as he observed signs of a very close correspondence going on between Sykes and a serving-wench, while he was preparing for his throw.

Sykes said something, in reply, about the eyes of the young lady, who, with some confusion, fled from the room.

Let not the reader suppose that modesty led to this precipitate retreat. To secure him against such an error, let him learn that a Judas is to be discerned in the person of James Sykes; and the agent of a Judas in the pretty serving-maid.

Notwithstanding, such is the short-sightedness of humanity, that the game went on briskly, cordially, and merrily; and neither qualm nor presentiment announced to our hero that he would shortly be in the predicament of Cæsar when he uttered the renowned example of sublimity—"*Et tu Brute.*"

Yet so it happened. An old acquaintance of those who have perused these pages with the attention they merit—even the guardian of the Round-house again appears on the scene; and behold the illustrious Jack Sheppard for the first time in "durance vile."

A scene—a solemn scene—a scene of magisterial dignity followed. We will not attempt to describe it—we lack the power. Long may the inimitable "Boz" live to wear the mantle of his inspiration; and paint from nature the urbanity of magistrates and equity of law. Neither will we attempt to analyse the feelings of Sheppard as he felt himself beneath the fangs of constable and gaoler. The impression made by the hands of those worthies, be it recorded for the benefit of all who may desire information on the subject, resembles the electric touch of a cat's-paw, or the more repulsive caress of a bloated toad.

"Remanded!" was the first intelligible sound that reached the ears of our hero during the protracted examination; and with it came the cheering prospect of a night in the Roundhouse.

In quod for the first time! Alas for novices, criminal or religious! theirs is the charm, and theirs the inconvenience of novelty! All novel as it was, there was no welcome harmony in the music of creaking hinges that shut Jack from the world; or in the rumbling of bolts and clanking of keys, that threatened a most effectual interruption of love and plunder—the business and pleasure of his life.

There he was, however, with the four walls around him; the ceiling above, the floor beneath, and bitter

Mrs. Sheppard interceding with Kneebone to save her son.

CHAPTER XII.

WHILE Jack was thus acquiring fame by violating the commands, braving the authority, and eluding the vigilance of justice, little of consequence occurred in the dwelling of Mr. Kneebone. That gentleman continued to deal out ells of cloth to his customers, orations teeming with Jacobitism to his friends, occasional consolation to his ancient mistress, Mrs. Sheppard, and his customary obedience to the buxom lady his wife. As the second in the household, *Mrs. Kneebone's* proceedings during this interval, have a claim on our notice. With her usual generosity, she released her husband from the discharge of all conjugal duties, excepting the passive one—of obedience; and as nature will crave, and the appetites of a wife, generous as Mrs. Kneebone, must be satisfied, she conferred on Captain Hamilton the honours, enjoyments, and responsibility of husband *active*. This arrangement, as we have seen, did not altogether escape the notice of the worthy woollen-draper. There were, however, various reasons that prevented him from exclaiming against this encroachment on his rights. First and foremost stood the great obstacle—Captain Hamilton was the better man of the two, and in its train flocked hundred accessary motives. Mr. Knee-bone's youth was on the wane; the bottle had more charms than the wife, or was at least better adapted to the physical changes wrought by time on the person of the once-gallant Knee-bone. Besides, he had his tastes—his fancies, and they had strengthened with his age; the same inclinations that twenty years before raised Dolly Do-allthings from her station as maid of all work to a peculiarly close intimacy with her master, disqualified him for a due appreciation of the attractions of his lawful wife, and in some degree justified that lady's jealousy of her lord's *ci devant* mistress—the mother of our hero. But to quicken the plot of our domestic comedy it must be re-corded, that this apparent resignation of his rights did not proceed from an inward approval of the conduct of the parties. Far be it from us to cast so dishonourable an imputation on any worthy linen-draper between St. Paul's and Charing-cross. No! Mr. Knee-bone was a man of honour, a man of delicate sentiment, a man of sensitive feeling. The success of the gallant captain aroused his indignation and lacerated his heart; but Mr. Kneebone wanted spirit, and all the measures his awakened ire and wounded sensibilities could induce him to take amounted to an occasional blow of the fist, inflicted on his own person, on a part of the head from whence spring ornamental antlers in certain quadrupeds.

Did he, most unfortunate biped, dread a similar decoration for himself, and by those blows attempt to prevent its growth? This question history does not answer; but it is the only way in which the biographer can ac-count for this extraordinary mode of vengeance, exercised by Mr. Kneebone, on his own person.

Philosophers have cautioned us against despising the day of small and feeble things; let us not look then with contempt on this head thumping

of the deceived husband. The proud-est river in the world is a stream, a brook at its source; the passion that led to the sad fate of Desdemona took its date from the enquiry "What dost thou think, Iago?" and all that is lamentable and tragical in the loves of Mrs. Kneebone and the Jacobite captain sprung from that apparently in-significant action, a thump of the head. We have seen in a previous part of this history the use *Jonathan Wild* deter-mined to make of Kneebone, and that the growing partiality of his spouse and Hamilton seemed to assist the working of his scheme. The exploits of Jack Sheppard brought the thief-taker and the woollen-draper now and then into connexion; and we doubt not that the former, with his usual quick sight, ob-served and accounted for the barbarous blows inflicted by the latter on his too fertile brows. Be this as it may,—whether thumps, or signs it is ambigu-ous,—it gave Wild an insight into the household of Mrs. Kneebone; an in-sight he obtained,—and resolved to turn to advantage the conjugal con-fusion. What steps he took—how he transported the intelligence gained at the tea-table of the draper, to the ca-binet of the Secretary of State—we have neither the means nor the pene-tration to discover; but his purpose he achieved, and, thanks to the thumps of the husband, the complaisance of the wife, the imprudence of the lover, and the diligent knavery of Jonathan, a blow threatened the establishment in the Strand, but little less fatal in its consequences to the parties concerned than the blow which threatened the Parliament house a few reigns before would have proved to the individuals for whom Guy Fawkes and Co. had arranged an aerial excursion of an exceedingly novel and expeditious na-ture.

Matters were in this state, one fine afternoon in the month of May, when Mr. and Mrs. Kneebone were sitting together in a little back parlour, behind their shop in the Strand, and looking for all the world as coy as the happiest man and wife in existence. The husband was busily engaged in examining his books, and felt considerable satisfaction at the prospect of finding at the end of the year a handsome balance in his favour; while the lady was embroidering something too large for a purse, and outrageously fine for a nightcap, but which was nevertheless destined fer the favoured captain. Just as she was thinking what an exceedingly *nice* man the captain was, and what an exceedingly *kind* man Mr. Kneebone was, her attention was drawn towards the shop by the entrance of a customer. It may be as well to state, that Mrs. Kneebone did not at all trouble herself about customers on ordinary occasions, but this afternoon every step threw her into a flutter, Captain Hamilton being expected to make one at their tea-table.

"Is it a customer, Mrs. K.?" asked her husband.

"I suppose so, my dear;—a shabby looking woman. But Francis is attending to her."

"Oh!" said the husband, and re-sumed his writing; the wife her embroidery.

"Mr. Kneebone is very busy, my good woman," said Francis Esdaile, who, under the happy auspices of his employer, had become a very useful, and a very handsome shopman; "I am afraid he cannot see you."

"Is his wife there?" said the woman, pointing to the little back room.

"Yes," said Francis, "I dare say she can see you," and, under ths influence of a good nature that taught him to treat the poor and unfortunate with kindness, he was going to summon his mistress.

"Not her—not her," cried the female, in a low but earnest whisper, "not for the world would I see her. But if you can procure me an interview with Mr. Kneebone, unknown to his wife, I shall be very much obliged—indeed I shall."

"I fear it is impossible."

"Lord! Lord! What shall I do?" exclaimed the poor creature, sinking on a chair that stood near, for the accommodation of customers, "What will become of me? My poor child! my dear, dear Jack!"

Francis caught the last word, and a host of recollections came to his mind, —his preserver in the fray at the Mint, —his kind companion when he first was put under the care of Mr. Kneebone,— the hardened boy, whose fate he pitied, while he reprobated his conduct—Jack Sheppard his playmate, formed the chief objects of them all. Could it be Jack's mother who stood before him?

"Are you Mrs. Sheppard?" asked Francis.

The woman started from her seat.

"You knew my boy?—you are Frank Esdaile whom he saved. Ah! he always liked you. You will not turn against him now he is in distress?"

"What has become of Jack?" asked Esdaile, eagerly, and apprehensive of the worst.

"They have him," replied the woman, frantically. "My poor, poor lad! But Mr. Kneebone will speak in his favour—will find him bail. I must see Mr. Kneebone!"

Frank would have apprized his master, but it was unnecessary.

Carried away by her emotion, Mrs. Sheppard had spoken in loud tones, and they soon reached the ears of the draper's wife. Suspending her occupation, Mrs. Kneebone approached the glass door looking into the shop, aud observed the speakers with attention. The appearance of the female denoted the most abject wretchedness. Her tattered garments bore witness to poverty and indolence; but there was an agony depicted on her countenance that drew pity from those who were most disgusted by her dissipated air. Mrs. Sheppard had indeed experienced that terrible change of thought and feeling, which those of her caste must ever experience, when the last meretricious charm of their course of life subsides, and leaves a prospect of cheerless unremediable misery. Nor was this all, she was a *mother*, and the spurned and withered harlot had to mourn a son exposed to the felon's brand and fate, a victim at once to her folly and neglect. We are apt to ascribe no feelings to those who have long indulged in vicious courses; alas! their own vices have formed within the breast the elements of a volcano of grief and passion, waiting but the hour of misfortune to vent forth its terrible eruption.

"As I live, Mrs. Sheppard!" thought Mrs. Kneebone. A moment more sufficed to convince her that she was not labouring under an error; the door was then thrown open, her husband aroused from his employment, and an explosion followed, too fierce to be described by our pen.

Mrs. Sheppard's errand was to seek the interference of Mr. Kneebone in behalf of her son, who, a short time after the escape recorded in our last chapter, had been again apprehended with Edgeworth Bess for a more serious robbery. In a few words, and those scarcely audible amidst the volley of abuse that fell from Mrs. Kneebone, she stated her object. The fury of the draper's wife redoubled. The excellence of woman is incomparable; but it is centred in her virtue: bereft of that palladium, she is open to the inroads of every vice. Fearful are the extremes to which passion will carry the licentious woman, and perhaps the most fearful of those lengths is the little compassion she feels for those, who, like her, have fallen into error and misfortune. Mrs. Kneebone, as erring as the mother of our hero, felt no compassion for her wretchedness, and insisted on her leaving the house unheard. The poor woman turned towards Mr.

Kneebone with a look of frantic entreaty; it was her last resource for her child, her boy, and she could not abandon it for a little abuse. This importunity had on Mrs. Kneebone the effect of downright provocation.

"Do you hear the hussey? Do you see the brute, Mr. K.? She contradicts me, disobeys me! Out of the house this instant. Mr. Kneebone, why don't you order her out of your house, sir? It is your house. Pray am I to consider that you encourage these visits?"

"Well, my dear, what *can* I do," enquired the husband, who, what with fear of his wife, and some remaining affection for his mistress, found himself in a terrible dilemma; "What *can* I do?"

"Nothing, you silly old fool, nothing. I must send for a constable, I see."

"But my dear Mrs. K., the exposure—"

"I dont care a fig for the exposure: it is the only way to protect you from such tricks. See! the brute don't stir. Oh! I'll send for a constable—I certainly will: here, Janet, Janet!"

Janet came at her mistress's bidding, and was instantly despatched in search of an authority. In no way daunted by these steps towards the execution of the threat, Mrs. Sheppard supplicated the more vehemently for succour for her boy. The offence was serious, she said, but a word from a respectable person, from his former master, would shorten his imprisonment.

"And a pity it would be to let him out a moment sooner than the law awards," interposed Mrs. Kneebone. "It would only be exposing honest people to fresh annoyance from the young scape-grace."

"No! no!" cried Mrs. Sheppard, "Jack is *not* hardened; he will reform. I have been a bad mother, neglected my child: he got among thieves; is it a wonder they taught him to steal? But he will be punished, and it will teach him his error. Oh! speak a word for my poor boy. He will amend his ways, I'll answer for it."

By this time Janet and the constable were to be seen advancing towards the house, and Mr. Kneebone resolved to make another effort to induce the woman to leave quietly before his arrival.

"It will little avail, my good woman," he began—

"*Good woman!*" interrupted his wife, "*Good woman!*—I have no patience."

"Silence, my dear. Allow me to convince Mrs. Sheppard how vain all interference on my part will prove. Sorry I am that a lad, once an inmate of my house, should have come to this pass. I hoped, after his escape from the Round House, he would have taken more care of himself: but no, you see how he acts, every day worse and worse. Really, Mrs. Sheppard, I despair of your son."

"*Your* son!" burst forth the distressed mother, with a violence that surprized all present. Hitherto she had acted with moderation; she had trusted that the case of her Jack was not hopeless, but now that his father joined with the most indifferent, and most opposed, to pronounce his case hopeless, her rage knew no bounds. "Yes, *your* son, Kneebone, your own boy. If he be lost, the sin of his destruction will not rest on my head alone. God is merciful; and the seducer of his mother will be responsible for his share in the poor lad's guilt."

"Do you hear, Mr. Kneebone, do you hear, sir, and *don't* you deny, dont you *attempt* to deny, *can't* you deny the assertions of this impudent woman?" enquired the lawful wife.

The only reply to these questions was a violent jerk given by the person addressed to his wig; an action that most expressively announced the utter confusion of the individual performing it. Its signification was not lost upon the lady.

"I see, I see it all," she shouted, "It is I am the injured, abused, deceived, unfortunate wife. Oh! Kneebone, what a dreadful truth hath this woman revealed! Take her away. Out of my sight. Oh! I faint. Janet, Francis, I faint, I faint."

Fortunately for Mrs. Sheppard the lady persisted so obstinately in her intention to faint that Mr. Kneebone had ample time to strive to give her a word or two of consolation in the shape of a promise to do his best, and at the same time to favour her escape from the house, before the arrival of the constable.

It was with a heavy heart she took her way towards the new prison; but before she turned out of the Strand, she was called by some one behind her. On turning round she perceived Francis Esdaile.

"What has Jack been doing?" asked he, as they struck off into a narrow street.

Mrs. Sheppard detailed as well as she was able the particulars of her son's recent capture. Esdaile shook his head in despair as he listened to her story. It was indeed a case of great aggravation. Sheppard had effected the robbery under the pretence of aiding a person who supposed he had been robbed; and then, having taken flight, was recognized and seized, while in the act of bellowing most lustily, "Stop thief," after the imaginary robber.

"Poor Jack," said Francis. "It grieves me to hear this: he was a good playfellow. But you must be in want, Mrs. Sheppard, and your son will require money in confinement. Here are my few savings—take them; it's all I can do for him."

"Heaven bless you!"

"Not a word. I am wanted at the shop. Farewell." And he bounded out of sight, leaving the poor widow astonished at his kindness.

Esdaile stole softly back into the shop, hoping that his absence had not been perceived. He found that Mrs. Kneebone had retired to calm, with the assistance of Janet, the perturbation of mind excited by the unexpected discovery she had made that afternoon. Ladies in a similar situation, may, perhaps, be curious to know to what means this illustrious specimen of her sex had recourse to, for comfort, on that trying occasion. Be it known, that she repaired to her chamber, and thought very seriously over a daring proposal, made to her by the captain, a day or two before. The schemes of Jonathan Wild had got wind, and Hamilton understood that danger attended his stay in London. By this time however, he was too enamoured of Mrs. Kneebone, to think of a separation, and had ventured, by way of reconciling the difficulty, to propose an elopement. This proposition was, at the time, received with all the indignation that became the person to whom it was addressed; but the events of that afternoon had greatly altered her determination.

"I am really driven to it," she said with a sigh, and immediately began an inspection of her dresses and trinkets that looked very much like a projected departure. Her next and most effectual mode of comfort was a very scrupulous attention to the duties of her toilet. What a balm for a torn heart did the rouge and the washes prove on that very memorable evening. Every stern emotion was driven from her heart as the adornment of her person advanced, and when completed, the serenity within might be conceived by the neatness and finery without.

During this operation her husband was conversing with a gentleman below; and Esdaile, having entered the shop, became unavoidably acquainted with their conversation.

"He comes here to night, you say?" asked Jonathan Wild, for he it was who addressed Mr. Kneebone.

"Yes, by the appointment of my wife."

"Ha! ha! ha! Then he falls into his own trap. I hold the warrant for his arrest."

"You rejoice me. I hope there is no harm between the man and my wife; but he does so feed her vanity, and set her on against me, that there is no bearing it."

"You will be rid of him to-night; never fear."

"But may they not suspect I have a hand in it? He may resist too, and cause a scuffle."

"Keep out of the way, man, if you are afraid."

"True, so I can; I can keep out of the way. I never thought of that."

A few more words passed between them, which Esdaile did not hear distinctly. For a moment he thought they related to himself; but not recognizing Jonathan, he dismissed the thought as absurd. The last words of Wild, however, as he left the shop, renewed his suspicions. When he turned from Kneebone to quit the shop, his eye rested upon Esdaile, who till then had passed unobserved. The significant look he immediately gave the draper did not escape the notice of the young man, nor the few words which accompanied it.

"We may do something for him yet," said Wild.

"Do, do," retorted the other; "and take my word for it, it will be the best action you ever did. He is a worthy lad—a very worthy lad."

With these words they separated. This interview caused young Esdaile many and painful thoughts during the rest of the afternoon. The events of his own history, and the fate of his companion were neither of them very cheerful; yet they presented an attraction that most effectually prevented his attending to the flirtations of Janet, who made repeated attempts to draw the young shopman into a conversation upon the events of the day.

"Only to think, Mr. Francis,—Jack Sheppard the son of our master!"

"Stranger things than that happen, Janet."

"To be sure—there's no knowing who you may turn out to be."

"Jack's twin brother, perhaps," said Esdaile, laughing.

"Oh! no, Mr. Esdaile, you are too good-looking for that."

"You compliment, Janet."

"No, no, I tell the truth. Do you think old Kneebone could be the father of such a nice-looking young man as you are? No, no. Never tell me. If you were to say Captain Hamilton, now, and missus, it would be a different thing, and much more probable."

"By-the-bye, Janet, is the captain expected here this evening?"

"Yes — if they had said nothing about it, I should have guessed what is in the wind. Bless you, for the last three hours I have done nothing but tie and untie, pin and unpin, in order to make missus fit to be seen, as she calls it."

"So," replied Francis to this speech of the Abigail, relapsing suddenly into silence, in order to discover, if possible, the connexion between this intelligence and the conversation he had overheard.

Janet, however, was not remarkable for her attachment to laconics, and the emphatic "So" was far from meeting with her approbation. An occasion soon presented itself of breaking the silence.

"Well I *never*!" exclaimed Janet.

Francis looked towards the little parlour to discover the cause of her surprise. Mr. Kneebone was observed through the open door brushing his beaver, pulling on his gloves, and performing other manœuvres that plainly indicated his intention to leave home.

"I never!" said Janet. "Just upon tea-time, as I'm alive; and master's a going out, though he knows the captain takes tea with missus this evening."

She was interrupted by the object of her remark, who walked into the shop, gave a few orders to Francis, and then very slowly stalked from the house.

Francis and Janet exchanged a look, and the latter resumed the discourse.

"'Tisn't at all to be wondered at that strange things happen, when old, and ugly, and faithless husbands go out, and leave a young and pretty wife to entertain very nice men at home. Do you think it is, Master Francis?"

The young man would have doubtless confirmed her opinion, but she was prevented from having that satisfaction by the appearance of the captain, whom she immediately ushered into the presence of the impatient Mrs. Kneebone. One circumstance, however, caused Janet some emotion. Francis, in some very expressive pantomime, intimated a wish that she would return immediately to the shop. What could he want, became a question of all-engrossing importance in the eyes of a maiden who had long wished to rank Esdaile among the number of her decided and declared admirers. To her mortification she had hitherto found Frank proof to her charms; it was, therefore, with the greatest delight, she perceived the least sign of an approach to the desired familiarity. She soon returned to her place, near Esdaile, and it was with some surprise she listened to the following enquiry:—

"Have you not slept, Janet, for the last night or two, in the back room of the first floor?"

Janet was thunderstruck. Mr. Esdaile, a modest young man, to begin in *that* way;—had he no respect for female modesty?

"You do not reply, Janet."

The poor maid was really at a loss. Her heart was quite inclined to give Esdaile all the information he could wish on the subject, but she could not divest herself of the policy which teaches the sex to make their conquest appear most difficult, when it is, in fact, already one.

"Why yes, Mr. Francis, I *have* slept there, the last night or two," she replied, employing every possible outward and visible sign of confusion and bashfulness, "and shall continue to sleep there."

"And pray, Janet, has not your chamber a door opening on the leads—a convenient kind of door, I mean, in cases of surprise?"

"Dear me! Dear me!" said the maid to herself, overcome by this sudden method of courting. "He not only comes to the point at once, but has taken necessary precautions beforehand. But this won't do—he flatters himself a great deal too much. I must let him know I consider it highly unbecoming a gentleman."

"Is it not as I say, Janet?" again enquired Francis, evidently impatient at the long pause between his question and its answer.

"Well, I must confess it is so," replied Janet, rather tartly, "and what *then*, sir?"

"Nothing: only it will just suit my purpose," said the young man, retiring behind a glass partition that divided off a part of the shop, bearing the name of the counting-house.

"Suit his purpose! Was there ever such impudence? And yet, perhaps, it is more ignorance and inexperience than anything else. Poor young man! What is he doing in there?" and Janet drew softly near the partition, raised herself on her ten toes till she was in a condition to observe plainly the actions of the young man.

"Writing, I declare. Explaining possibly his intentions. I really do like him. It was all awkwardness what he said just now. How he does write! How delicate! How attentive!"

A voice from the inner room now summoned Janet from love to duty. As she tripped away she consoled herself by saying,—

"I shall have it at tea-time—I dare say he will slip it into my hands on the sly."

Her castles in the air were soon to be overthrown. Before she had reached the end of the shop, Esdaile reappeared from the counting-house, and holding a note between his fingers, beckoned Janet towards him.

The summons was speedily obeyed by the delighted girl, though her heart beat violently at the prospect of an assignation.

"Janet, will you do me a favour?"

"I shall always be happy to serve you when I can, Mr. Francis."

"Then take this letter."

"That letter, Mr. Francis?"

"Yes; don't be afraid of it—it does not contain detonating powder."

"Are you sure it don't?" asked the soubrette, who, not exactly aware of the nature of detonating powder, thought that it might mean something reprehensible in an amatory epistle; "Well, in that case, I think I may consent to take it."

"And deliver it as directed, as privately and speedily as you can—there's my good Janet."

So saying Esdaile again retreated to the counting-house, and immersed himself in the mysteries of day-book and ledger.

"Can anything be more delicate—as directed—privately and speedily! Would not trust himself, even to mention my name. How he must love me to be sure. But what does he say?" And she began to turn over the letter, first looking at the seal; this, however, presented no interest, bearing for an inscription the letter K, commercial signet for the house of Kneebone. The address next claimed her notice; there would surely be something pretty in the address.

"How is this!" exclaimed the indignant maid. "To Captain Hamilton! What have I to do with Captain Hamilton? I won't take his letter, that I won't. An impudent varlet! To ask me questions about my bed-room, and then make me his lackey—I'll serve him out for this! What does he want with Captain Hamilton, unknown to

Jack Sheppard breaking out of Clerkenwell Prison and liberating Edgeworth Bess.

my mistress I should like to know? I deliver his letter *privately ?* Not such a flat as all that either. Missus shall see it, and then, if all isn't right, *we* shall see, Mr. Jackanapes."

With this invective Janet gained the presence of her mistress, who was immediately favoured with a perusal of the billet. The effects it produced, however, was very contrary to the wishes of the abigail, as she was immediately dismissed from the apartment.

"Read that," said Mrs. Kneebone.

The note was as follows :—

"Captain Hamilton,

Danger awaits you. A warrant is issued against you---will be served this evening, in this house. I fear you

No. 11.

have been watched to the house, and cannot leave it in safety. Should you receive a signal from me, fly to the back room of the first floor : a door leads from thence to the leads, and by descending into the court you may perhaps escape.

Francis Esdaile."

"This is no false alarm," cried the captain."

"Say not so, my dear Hamilton,"

"Alas! Why should I deceive you. The advice of Esdaile must be followed. We must part, dearest."

As for the scene that ensued, we must beg the reader to call to mind all that he may have read in *pathetics,* and to assure him that it surpassed every thing of the kind in the same proportion as the sensibilities of the individuals concerned surpassed the sensibilities of other people. The results, however, were sensibly felt in the family; first by Janet, who was suddenly bolted out of the apartment; secondly by Esdaile, who looked in vain for his customary potations of tea ; and lastly, by Jonathan Wild and Mr. Kneebone, the one having lost his prize, and the other his encumbrance.

There was one dire effect of this elopement, however, which it is incumbent upon us to make obvious to the reader; it in no wise disposed Jonathan Wild to favour Esdaile. It will be remembered that the thief-taker alone possessed a clue to the family of the foundling. These documents he treasured up with a store of others, which, by leading to the detection of real or pretended criminals, and transferring property from supposed to rightful owners, or vice versa, furnished him with incalculable resources against the day of adversity. Francis, however, could have no claim on Wild's protection, since the latter traced the flight of Hamilton to a warning given by Esdaile, whom he remembered had been present in the shop while he conferred with Kneebone.

While Esdaile was thus exposing himself to the wrath of Jonathan Wild, Jack Sheppard was earning for himself new laurels within the walls of the New Prison. It was with a heavy heart Mrs. Sheppard, on parting with Francis, proceeded to visit her son. As she counted over the little she owed to the generosity of the foundling, she glanced from time to time at the different shops, hoping to find some article that might prove acceptable to the prisoner. It is a terrible thing for a parent to have to propitiate a son; yet such was the position of this unhappy woman.

"On whom can he reflect," she thought, "but on me, as the author of his ruin. By me was he brought unprovided for into a miserable world; by me was he suffered to follow every bent of a mind naturally too wayward; by me,"---and the poor wretch leant against an adjoining doorway as the thought came to her mind---"by me was he trained for the gallows."

When she recovered from her momentary agitation her eye was attracted by the objects around. She stood near the doorway of a furniture broker. Among the motley ware exposed for sale, her anxious eye rested on a basket of tools. There was something in the bright blades, and saws, and files glittering before her in the spring sunshine, that cheered her heart. Her spirits quickly revived; he might escape. In a minute the bargain was struck ; a chisel and a file were carefully concealed beneath her bosom, and she hastened on to the dungeon of her boy.

In the meanwhile, heavily fettered, in the strongest ward of the prison, and thence called Newgate Ward, sat Jack Sheppard, and not far from him, the person who at that time seemed the sole object for whom the few good feelings he possessed were served—Edgeworth Bess. The attachment of the housebreaker and his doxy had its romance, though no elegance marked the expression of their sentiments. A little incident will confirm this.

When captured, they were both penniless, and borne off to different cells in the lock-up house. From a sister-prostitute Bess contrived to raise a few pence, and the whole were immediately despatched to Jack. The next day they were committed ; and, as may be supposed, after a night of fasting and watching, were both in a miserable plight. Some circumstance gave rise to a dispute about money.

"What did you do with the pence I sent you last night, Jack ?" enquired Bess.

"Bought some baccy," was the reply.

"You did very right, Jack," retorted the wench: her countenance, haggard through exhaustion, for a moment illuminated by an expression of satisfaction, which plainly told he had obliged her most by taking care of himself.

But to return to the prison. They sat almost in silence, for each was dejected. To Bess, the idea of an escape never occurred; she would have deemed it as practicable to leave the limits of earth, or cleave through the sky, as to make a passage through the place of their confinement. Far other thoughts occupied the mind of her companion. From the moment he first felt the weight of the fetters on his arms, and gave a surly glance at the walls around him, one thought took possession of his brain, secured the most intense application of his mind, became the subject of his mid-day reveries, of his midnight dreams — the thought of escape. To show the thorough difference of the minds of the prisoners, how the one accommodated itself to suffering, while the other rose above every obstacle, we will report a short conversation that took place between them, somewhere about the fourth day of their imprisonment.

Bess began. She exclaimed with an oath that she was weary of her life —ready to die.

"Thought so," said Jack, with a taunting indifference.

"D—n you for a tame, quiet, contented thief!" retorted the lady. "How in the name of h—l do you contrive to be so blasted patient?"

"I think," said Jack.

"Lord a mercy! Think. The devil's in it if thinking don't make me a bloody sight worse. What the devil do you think about?"

"Escape," replied Jack, making his fetters clank till the passages of the prison echoed again, as he spoke.— Widely different as their natures were, so was the expression the word *escape* brought to the countenance of either; confidence sat on the features of Sheppard, incredulity on those of Bess.

"Pooh!" she exclaimed, and turned from him with a profound contempt at so absurd a project, and at the same time giving the place a more minute survey than she had yet done. It did not at all abate her incredulity. The doors were massive, the walls thick; the window was the only possible outlet, but this aperture was small, divided too, by a solid bar of oak, at least nine inches thick, and moreover, guarded by strong bars of iron; besides, it was a great height from the ground, and a wall, nearly as high, rose as if to exclude hope, directly before them, on the other side.

"Escape," added Jack, watching the movement of Bess's eyes, and guessing her thoughts. "Who raised these walls, Bess, come? Who constructed the little place in which we are confined? Man. And who has man enclosed in it? His fellow. 'Tis but a fair match—man to man." And he struck a light air, beating time with the chains, as though defying their weight to shackle his mind.

"You seem *happy*, Jack," said Bess, in an envious tone.

"I should be with one or two things, Bess."

"And what are they?"

"A file and a chisel."

Again the lady would have displayed her indignation, but they were interrupted.

"A visitor," said the gaoler, and Jack confronted his mother.

There was much surliness in his deportment towards Mrs. Sheppard, and while she made no complaint, it seemed no slight addition to her misery.

"Have you brought me money?" asked he. "We can do nothing here without it."

In silence, and with much trembling, for fear of detection, Mrs. Sheppard conveyed her purchase into the hands of her son. His thrill of delight as he concealed it about his person, did not escape her notice. It was a short moment of happiness to her wretched heart. With a gaze full of affection, she kept her eyes fixed upon him, and met his as she withdrew. Another pleasure was reserved for her. She had won a way to her son's heart, by discovering and gratifying his inmost wish, for a tear twinkled in the house-breaker's eye. Alas! poor mother. If there is any feeling in the world as full of joy and as passing as love, it is a mother's delight at a glimpse of excellence in a profligate son.

At two o'clock the next morning, all slept in the prison, save our hero and his companion. The time had been well employed since the last visit of the inspector. The bar of oak and the bars of iron were removed from the window, and thrown in disorder on the floor. A blanket and sheet, securely fastened, swung from the opening, and pointed an easy descent to the ground. Bess, divested of her gown, had tried without success to pass through.

"Come, off with that, lass," said Jack, pointing to her petticoat.

"But decency, Jack."

"D—n decency. Who is there to see but me; and I shan't make any discoveries I guess?"

The scrupulous damsel, satisfied by these arguments, disrobed; and very shortly, aided by her unwieldy person, reached the ground. Another difficulty, of a nature so serious as to threaten the failure of their project, arose in the opposite wall. Bess trembled, and Jack worked; a scaling ladder was soon contrived, and the adventurous couple found themselves at liberty. Before day-break Jack was once more free.

CHAPTER XI.

NOTHING could exceed the astonishment of Mr. Kneebone when he learnt, on his return home in the evening, the sudden departure of Captain Hamilton and his wife. He expected to hear of the apprehension of the former, and rehearsed, during his walk, a reply to the invectives he felt sure of receiving from his amiable lady. That he should find her gone too, never once entered his head; had it done so, he would have been saved a great deal of anxiety; for he looked forward with no small degree of terror to the stormy reception he expected from Mrs. Kneebone. Fortunately for Francis, who also expected blame for the share he had taken in their flight, Jonathan Wild had left town in pursuit of the fugitives, and the worthy draper had not sufficient penetration to discover in his apprentice the individual who had given this unexpected turn to his plot against Hamilton. But we learn, in time, to resign ourselves to the worst of evils; and Mr. Kneebone was not so destitute of philosophy as to break his heart for the loss of a wife. Esdaile, who considered himself as the remote cause of this calamity, was therefore rejoiced to see his master rise manfully above his misfortune, and resume his usual occupations as though nothing had transpired. The want of a female to superintend the little household was indeed soon felt; and loudly did the deserted husband complain that he had never before found himself so cheerlessly situated in a domestic point of view. He would even at times refer to the days of Dolly Do-allthings; a subject on which his fear of Mrs. Kneebone's ire had for many years kept him silent.

"Why don't you recall Dolly?" said Francis to him a few days after his loss; "I am sure it would be a great charity, for Mrs. Sheppard looks as if she were starving."

"Do you really think I ought, Francis?"

"When I consider what passed between you in the shop the other day, I should say you are in duty bound to provide for her, sir."

"I think you are right, Francis."

Here the conversation closed, but the idea was acted upon; and, in a few days, Mrs. Sheppard was reinstated in the place she had occupied when Miss Dolly Doallthings.

In the mean time Jack Sheppard and Bess were making the most of their liberty. Old haunts were visited with the most rash daring, and old acquaintances renewed with the greatest eagerness. Jack's imprisonment, among other inconveniences, had not increased his finances; and the loving couple soon found themselves reduced to the necessity of resuming their suspended avocations. With this view, Jack repaired one morning to the river-side, in the hope of meeting with some stray article or other belonging to the numerous travellers arriving at, or leaving the metropolis. He was not long on the look out before a lady and gentleman, engaged in earnest conversation, drew near; and, from the deep interest they seemed to take in the subject of discourse, promised to become an easy prey to the depredations of the thief. Eagerly did Jack approach them; but the gentleman turning suddenly round, said—

"My good lad, do you know of any vessel about to sail for Holland?"

Sheppard returned a brief answer to this question, and turned hastily away. It was time he did so, for the lady was no other than Mrs. Kneebone, his former mistress, and her companion the Jacobite captain. Scarcely were they out of sight, than Jack was again accosted; and this time he trembled in good earnest, for he was now addressed by the notorious thieftaker Jonathan Wild. Jonathan, however, had too important business on hand, the arrest of a Jacobite, to waste time on a common felon. He confined, therefore, his enquiries to what concerned Captain Hamilton.

"They were enquiring after a vessel bound for Holland," said Jack.

"The very thing: curse me if I am not in luck. You have given me valuable information, and I shall not forget the service. They went this way, you said?"

"Yes; you can't fail to overtake them."

Wild darted off at a swift pace, and soon caught sight of the fugitives. A slight alteration in his dress, effected in the parlour of a publichouse, converted him into the master of a vessel, and in a few minutes he stood before them in that capacity. Among the many extensive systems of which Jonathan was the author and centre, was a plan for conveying stolen property to a foreign market, where it might be disposed of without fear of detection. For this purpose he purchased and fitted out a merchant vessel, which, on that day, happened to be waiting in the river for a fair wind. A scheme, then, for securing both the fugitives was instantly formed. Eager to leave England, the captain offered the pretended master of the vessel his own price for a passage to Holland; and we need not say that the negociation was met with the same alacrity by the other party. On board they went; the ship was got under weigh; but, at the mouth of the river, the loving exiles were separated—Captain Hamilton for the shore and a state-prison, the lady to remain on board for the pleasure of a new admirer, even Mr. Jonathan Wild. We will not describe the means he employed to carry his point—it will be sufficient to say that he was eminently successful. Mrs. Kneebone, finding herself without either husband or lover, received very gratefully all the consolation Jonathan was disposed to offer in her destitute state.

These occurrences soon reached the ears of our hero; who, in the midst of an active life where every day brought new adventures, still found time to enquire occasionally after the condition of his former friends. Toward Mr. Kneebone he never bore any very friendly feeling: he remembered the use that gentleman had once made of his authority as master, and how obstinately he had refused all interference in his behalf during his recent imprisonment. Jack was conscious that, in his turn, he now possessed the power of annoying; and he determined, the first opportunity, to take summary vengeance on the woollen-draper. To facilitate his success in the arduous profession of housebreaker, he left no means unemployed likely to ensure that end; and about this time was at great pains to secure, as accomplices, the servants and apprentices of those whom he proposed to rob. One Anthony Lamb easily fell in with this design. Pleased with the housebreaker's friendly bearing—fired by the account of his exploits, the unwary tool gave him every information necessary for the robbery of Mr. Carter, a mathematical instrument maker, and the former master of the corrupted apprentice. This affair turned out very successful. The thieves bore off property to the amount of three hundred pounds, besides expensive clothes from the wardrobe of a tailor, who lodged in the house. With the assistance of the latter spoils our hero turned a fine gentleman. The costume of a beau graced the limbs of the housebreaker, and proved so effectual a disguise as to deceive his most intimate associates.

He did not, however, allow this genteel comedy to divert his attention from the business of real life. The dwelling of Mr. Kneebone continued to excite his cupidity, and his deep dislike for an old master his revenge. It was a design, however, that could not be effected alone; and Jack's first step was to communicate this new project to a few chosen confederates, and among them, Anthony Young was honoured with his confidence. Scarcely was the young apprentice admitted to share the honours of this attack, than he was detected as a partner in the burglary committed on the premises of Mr. Carter. An ample confession saved him from the worst consequences of his crime, and he was sentenced to transportation.

"Francis, Francis," cried Mr. Kneebone, one morning, soon after Esdaile had handed him a letter; "Francis, I say!"

"Here I am, sir," said the young man, running to the side of his master, who was leisurely taking his breakfast in the little back parlour.

"And Mrs. Sheppard—where is Mrs. Sheppard?" continued the old man, in evident agitation. "I want Mrs. Sheppard."

The ci-devant maid of all work, now honoured with the title of housekeeper, was forthwith called; and both housekeeper and shopman stood anxious to know the pleasure of their lord and master.

"I'm going to be robbed," said he.

"Robbed!" echoed both his servants.

"Read," rejoined the draper, placing before them an ill-scrawled dirty note.

It contained, indeed, information to that effect, urging Mr. Kneebone to be on his guard; but no signature explained the source of such intelligence.

"Who can it be?" said the two servants.

"Aye, who can it be?" enquired their master; and the triumvirate discussed every suggestion presenting itself to their minds.

Mrs. Sheppard, like a sanguine mother, hoped that Jack, retaining a regard for his old master, had been apprised of the intention of some thieves, and adopted this means to frustrate their plan. It would be impossible to describe how fondly the mother clung to any shadow of good in her boy.

Mr. Kneebone, with the conscience of a tyrant, sensible of having made undue usage of his power, could not forget that he had rendered himself obnoxious to the house-breaker, and at once guessed the real source from whence the project of robbing his house emanated; Esdaile had similar suspicions, though he found some difficulty in bringing himself to think so ill of Sheppard, and forbore expressing them, out of respect to the unhappy mother.

The anonymous letter came from Sheppard's new victim, the apprentice Anthony Lamb.

"What is to be done?" said Mr. Kneebone, concluding that to take measures of defence would be a more profitable employment of time than idle suggestions as to the source of the evil they apprehended.

"We must be on the watch," replied Francis.

"And inform the patrol," added Mrs. Sheppard, while Mr Kneebone closed the proceedings by d——g the thieves for making him the subject of their exploits.

The night-of the stated day found the different inmates at the posts assigned to them, and as alert as the occasion required. Mrs. Sheppard was not the least vigilant. Her maternal affection would not allow her for a moment to consider her son as the instigator of the robbery, and having learnt the suspicions of Mr. Kneebone, she felt the more anxious to convince him of his error. Nothing, she thought, could do this so effectualy as the apprehension of the thieves, should they make the attempt; and accordingly, Mrs. Sheppard resolved to leave nothing undone that might lead to their discovery. She took her station at a door that appeared the most likely to be fixed on for their entrance, and from that post listened with anxiety to every voice or footfall that resounded through the deserted street. At length sounds were heard approaching her place of concealment; agitated and breathless, she endeavoured to learn from what they proceeded. She could not be mistaken—they were footsteps, cautious footsteps, yet the heavy footsteps of men. They drew nearer; she heard voices; and though they spoke in a low whisper, a word now and then reached her ear.

"Hist!" said one man. "They are not yet in bed: the light we observed in one window has been removed to another."

"Not in bed at this hour?" exclaimed another; "then we are watched."

"God be praised!" ejaculated Mrs. Sheppard; "it is not my son's voice," and she was on the point of giving an alarm that must inevitably have led to their capture, had not a few more words from another speaker kept her motionless.

"'Tis time to be off then, my lads" said Jack Sheppard, in a louder and more daring tone than the rest. "D——n the old codger; we'll do for him yet, lads, and have three hnndred pounds of his money."

The poor mother listened with horror to a voice she knew too well, and it deprived her of all power to give an alarm. Retreating footsteps were heard soon after, and the silence of the night again reigned in the street.

A few nights passed away, but as no renewed attempt was made, Mr. Kneebone considered the letter as a hoax. Esdaile and Janet supported him in that opinion, and censured the obstinancy with which Mrs. Sheppard persisted to keep watch; but Dolly knew the perseverance of her son—with what undaunted energy he prosecuted an enterprise once conceived; and in this case she feared that motives of enmity towards Mr. Kneebone, as well as the great amount of booty, would increase rather than diminish his firmness of purpose. To disclose the discovery she had made on a preceding night, and betray her son, was a course she could not resolve on adopting; but she hoped, by incessant watchfulness, to defeat the design of the robbers, protect the property of her master, and secure her son from detection. Under the influence of these good feelings, she was prepared for long and wearisome vigils; vigils she took care should remain a secret to the rest of the family. A repetition of such exertion could not, however, fail to exhaust, and one night sleep overcame her, long before the clock of the new church had gone one. She had, by some oversight, forgotten to renew her candle; when, therefore, a noise in the lower part of the house broke on her troubled slumbers, she found herself in total darkness. She paused to satisfy herself that the noise she had heard was not imaginary —part of a forgotten dream. The slow creaking of a door convinced her that her fears were not unfounded; thieves were in the house, and notwithstanding their caution, she heard enough to convince her they were well acquainted with the premises, and were swiftly approaching the room in which Mr. Kneebone slept. These circumstances, taken in connexion with what she had before overheard, left no room to doubt but that her own son was the ringleader of the party. She felt that no time was to be lost in reaching the scene of theft; but what steps to take —how betray a son—how leave exposed to the injury of ruffians, a master, more than a master, a husband in the sight of heaven—the father of her child. Terrible was the penalty she paid for a youth of crime and folly in that brief moment of suspense. Scarcely knowing what she did—more guided by instinct than by reason, she flew towards the apartment of Mr. Kneebone, but with so light a step that not the least sound intimated her approach to the robbers. There were two doors to the room, one opening on the landing, another into a small closet communicating with an adjoining room used as a ware-room. On descending the stairs she heard the door on the landing place close gently, and concluded the thieves had entered by it. To gain the other door was the work of a moment; and she succeeded in opening it

without alarming the gang. She almost sunk to the floor with terror at the sight she beheld. Two men were engaged in ransacking a chest of drawers, and were indistinctly seen by the glimmer of their dark lanterns. The curtains of the large old-fashioned bedstead, while they concealed her from view, prevented her seeing Mr. Kneebone. The reflection of a lantern, held at some height on the other side of the bed, convinced her, however, that he was an object of attentive consideration to one of the robbers. In neither of the other thieves did she recognise her son. She drew near to the bed, and placing her eye to a small aperture in the hangings, tried to discover what passed. The light held by the third thief fell on the features of the sleeping man, while his own were almost concealed in the shade. To the mother, however, they were sufficiently apparent; it was her son, and the pistol he held pointed at *his father's* head. It was with difficulty she suppressed a scream of horror.

"Make haste," said one of the men examining the drawers—"the old blade may wake."

"Take your time, lads," said Jack with a frightful coolness: "D—n him, if he does wake, or we should be surprised, I'll blow his brains out for him."

As he spoke his eye rested on the aperture through which Mrs. Sheppard gazed: she quailed beneath his glance. Had he discovered her, and was it a threat he held out? The poor woman had no alternative: inwardly praying that no blood might be shed, she watched the thieves continue their depredations, nor left the bed-side of her master until sure that her son was out of the house, and beyond the danger of discovery, to which his rash enterprise exposed him. This robbery proved productive to our hero, but it hastened the catastrophe by which he ended his days.

Some time elapsed, and little com-

Sheppard drinking the St. Giles's bowl on his way to Tyburn.

munication took place between the principal parties figuring in our history. Sheppard varied his business as burglar with an occasional excursion in the capacity of highwayman, though they seldom extended further than Hampstead. In exploits of this nature his time passed to his heart's content, until he was apprehended for the robbery committed on the premises of Mr. Kneebone, through the means of Edgeworth Bess, who discovered to Jonathan Wild the place of his retreat.

. This time his imprisonment took a more serious aspect than on any former occasion. He was tried, condemned, and the court left him no hope of mercy. It may be supposed that the spirit which had so boldly contrived the means of escape on former occasions, would not

desert him in this emergency. In that hopeless sojourn the condemned hole, with nine others as wretched though less daring than himself, he thought and dreamt of flight; and having procured some implements, imparted the design to his "*companions in tribulation.*" These men, however, lost all courage in the near prospect of death; while Sheppard, relying on his ingenuity, braved it when nearest and most formidable. To accomplish his end, he left unemployed no resource that accomplished duplicity could possess. He listened to the exhortations of the chaplain with attention and apparent gratitude.

"I will follow your advice," said he, "and *prepare.*"

How successfully he prepared to meet

the fatal moment the following facts will show.

On the Monday previous to the Friday fixed for his execution, he conversed merrily for hours together with various friends, among them his favourite Bess, who had somewhat fallen in his affections since his last capture at the door of the condemned cell. Towards the close of the day a favourable moment presented itself—a moment that the dexterity of Sheppard alone could have turned to account. While some individuals were, in the lodge, conversing on the subject of his wonderful escape from the New Prison, he gave them the slip, and was for the third time free.

Sheppard now enjoyed a reputation that must have proved exceedingly annoying to a man in his situation. The different enquiries made by those in pursuit of him, the accounts of his adventures and escapes published in the journals, made every one acquainted with his history. He could enter no place of public resort without hearing his name, the censure of the old—the astonishment of the young; execrated by the *godly*, and praised by all admirers of dexterous ingenuity. Nor was this the most inconvenient circumstance connected with his position :—his person was almost as well known as his history. Portraits of Jack Sheppard met his view on every side : it formed a favourite subject for drawingroom engravings and cottage woodcuts.

Such a reputation went far to endanger his safety, and nothing but his ingenuity could have counteracted its influence. A fixed abode was out of the question : but with him that had never formed a leading feature in his comforts : and his costume was varied enough to satisfy the caprice of the most outrageous *masquer*. But there is no withstanding the tremendous force the law can bring into play against those who are under its ban. We might almost imagine its emissaries gifted with omniscience, so easily and surely do they penetrate every disguise ; with omnipresence as extensively as their influence felt. Against this force even the arm of Sheppard was impotent : he could escape from the dungeons it had erected ; but there was no refuge against the untiring activity of justice, or the cupidity of the hunters of human blood, retained, through necessity, in her pay. Jack was retaken.

Retaken, but not subdued. Fearlessly may we trust the incalculable resources of the human mind. With every new necessity occurs a new expedient, and despair alone can render useless the treasury of the invention. A darker dungeon and weightier fetters had no influence on Sheppard : he contrived new measures while his spiritual instructor conceived him engaged in holy meditation ; he turned over the leaves of his Bible, but he made its pages a receptacle for the prisoner's treasure, an old file. His projects being matured by frequent consideration, he chose his time. The Sessions came on, the engagements of the keepers would leave him leisure for his operations, and after the last visit for the day he began his toil. Incredible must have been the labour by which he broke his handcuffs, opened the padlock of his fetters, and removed an iron bar that, placed across the chimney, prevented his escape in that direction. Yet it was accomplished, and he entered the Red Room, whose door had been closed for seven years. More than six massive doors were passed successively, all locked and bolted, and some of them on the side contrary to the prisoner. Part of this arduous task was employed in the dark ; and as the chimes of St. Sepulchre's church went eight, he again breathed, from the upper leads of the prison, the fresh air. In order to effect a descent on the adjoining house it became necessary to procure a blanket from his cell. He retraced his steps, and undiscovered, but with a beating heart, returned—completed his work—and was no longer within the walls of Newgate.

He was now on the leads of a private house, and the garret window stood open. To pass through the house undetected was now his chief object; but at that hour of the evening, the shops yet open, the streets still thronged, the passage was not without danger: laughter from within, the murmur of the crowd from without, reached his ears. How little did the thousands uttering those sounds of life and activity dream of the situation of the branded housekeeper, who with trembling step, in darkness and solitude, descended the staircase of the turner's house. Some one was ascending — there was no time for retreat, and for a moment he thought of encountering the person with violence. A door left ajar on the landing seemed to offer greater seccuriy, and he entered. The room was occupied: a person by the bedside conversed with an invalid upon it. Fortunately for Jack, a screen was near, and on tip-toe he crept behind it.

"You will not then make this sacrifice, to ascertain the fate of the boy?" asked the man in health.

Jack shuddered as he listened. He knew the voice to be that of Jonathan Wild.

"No! no! I must and will expose —tell all. The poor child must be restored to his rights."

"Nonsense! The lad has learnt an honest business—is happy enough, as the shopman of a woollen-draper. Secrecy is the only condition on which I can let you know more. Farewell. I shall call to morrow, when I hope to find you in a different mind."

So saying, Wild withdrew. The moment was not to be lost. Sheppard felt he had some claims on the sick man's attention; the subject of their conversation clearly related to Francis Esdaile

He stole to the bedside, and raising the curtain, revealed himself to the invalid.

"In heaven's name, what do you want?" asked the sick man.

"Your silence," said Jack.

The man made an attempt to give an alarm, but Sheppard continued—

"You wish for information respecting Francis Esdaile?"

"I do, God knows I do—the poor wronged boy!"

"Give me concealment till I can safely leave the house, and I will put it into your power to communicate with him immediately."

The invalid rose with a violent effort. "I will," said he. "Oh, give me tidings of the lad—I shall yet see him restored to his rights."

Sheppard was not sorry at this incident, as it gave him an opportunity of benefiting Francis, for whom he felt a strong friendship. He related to the sick man all that he knew respecting Esdaile, and learnt in return, that the invalid had been a creature of Sir Luke Gascoigne, a great bad man, who had employed him to kidnap the child in order to secure to himself the enjoyment of an extensive property. On his death, and a prey to remorse, the wretch had sent for Jonathan Wild, hoping, through him, to gain tidings of the lost child. Jonathan, however, was retained by Sir Luke, and refused to discover the situation of Esdaile, but on the condition of strict secrecy.

These terms did not at all fall in with the design of the dying man, and he received with a pleasure amounting to rapture the proposition of our hero. Jack continued in the sick man's room till the family were at rest; he then put into his hands the address of Mr. Kneebone, and took his departure from the house.

Our history approaches its close, Sheppard's intemperance betrayed him for the last time, into the hands of justice. At the early age of twenty-three, after furnishing the whole kingdom with a subject of wonder and conversation, he suffered the penalty of the law at Tyburn, 16th November, 1724. On his way to the place of execution, he still maintained the hope of effecting an escape. Though his behaviour was grave and becoming, yet furtive glances at the crowd, and a word or two he let fall, confirmed the opinion, that he hoped to the last moment to evade the hand of justice.

"I have now," said he, "as great satisfaction of heart, as if I was going to enjoy an estate of a hundred a year."

The chaplain who attended him put a pious construction on these words; but from what had transpired between Sheppard and a person in whom he placed confidence, it appears they were not prompted by the housebreaker's piety. A friend had furnished him with a knife; and he entertained a design of cutting the cords which bound his hands together, and throwing himself among the crowd, as the cart passed the Little Turnstyle. He imagined the passage would favour his escape, being impassable to the officers, who were on horseback. As far as the crowd was concerned, he trusted to his popularity, or its sympathy, and doubted not to meet with assistance.

The examination of the prisoner's person in the press yard thwarted this purpose. The bleeding fingers of Watson, the officer, soon betrayed the opened knife, concealed in Sheppard's pocket.

This discovery did not, however, chase hope from his mind. He hoped under the very shadow of the gallows, even while vibrating with the rope; for he had requested his acquaintance to obtain his body as quickly as they could, and to employ every means to restore him to life.

The fatal moment could not, however, be retarded by his most sanguine prospects; the bowl of ale, with its infusion of marjorum, was offered, and drank according to the custom of the time. The cart passed from under him, and the housebreaker, with great difficulty, closed his short and busy career.

His remains were afterwards interred in St. Martin's churchyard.

Of those who have been connected with our hero, during this narrative of his life, we can only give a brief account. Mr. Kneebone continued, for many years, to enjoy the comforts of Mrs. Sheppard's housekeeping, who, thoroughly reformed, ended her days in peace. Francis Esdaile was restored to his connexions, his tit'e, and his fortune; and filled, for many years, situations of honor in the service of his country. Captain Hamilton was exiled for his share in the conspiracy of the time, and was honourable enough to offer an assylum to the woman he had ruined Jonathan Wild was hung.

Jack Sheppard wrote an account of his last escape from Newgate, and left it with the ordinary for publication. As this feat obtained great notoriety, our hero's own account of it will be an appropriate close to our narrative.

"As my last escape from Newgate, out of the strong room, called the Castle, has made a greater noise in the world than any other action of my life, I shall relate every minute circumstance thereof, as far as I am able to remember, intending thereby to satisfy the curious, and do justice to the ignorant.

"After I had been made a public spectacle for many days, with my legs chained together, loaded with heavy irons, and stapled down to the floor, I thought it was not altogether impracticable to escape, if I could be furnished with proper implements; but, as every person that came near me was carefully watched, there was no possibility of any such assistance; till one day, in the absence of my gaolers, looking about the floor I spied a small nail within reach; and with that, after a little practice, I found the great horse padlock that went from the chain to the staple in the door might be unlocked; which I did afterwards at pleasure, and was frequently about the room, and had several times slept on the barracks, when the keeper imagined I had not been out of my chair. But being unable to pass up the chimney, and void of tools, I remained where I was : till being detected in these practices by the keepers, who surprised me one day before I could fix myself to the staple in the manner they left me, I showed Mr. Pitt, Mr. Rouse, and Mr. Parry, my art; and before their faces unlocked the padlock with the nail; and, though people made such an outcry about it, there is scarce a smith in London but what may easily do the same thing; however, this called for a further security of me, for till now I had remained without handcuffs. A jolly pair was provided for me, and Mr. Kneebone was present when they were put on. I, with tears, begged his intercession to the keepers to preserve me from those dreadful manacles; telling him my heart was broken, and that I should be much more miserable than before. Mr. Kneebone could not refrain from shedding tears, and used his utmost endeavours with the keepers to keep me from them, but all to no purpose; on they went, though at the same time I despised them; and well knew that with my teeth only I could take them off at pleasure; but this was to lull them into a firm belief that they had effectually frustrated all attempts to escape for the future. I was still far from despairing. The turnkey and Mr. Kneebone had not been gone down stairs an hour ere I made an experiment and got off my handcuffs, and before they visited me again I put them on, and industriously rubbed and fretted the skin on my wrists, making them appear bloody, as thinking, if such a thing was possible to be done, not to move the turnkeys to compassion, but rather to confirm them in their opinion; but though this had no effect upon them, it wrought much more upon the spectators, and drew down from them not only much pity, but quantities of silver and copper; but I wanted still a more useful metal; a crow, a chisel, a file,

and a saw or two; those weapons being more serviceable to me than the mines in Mexico; but there was no expecting any such things in my circumstances.

"Wednesday, the 14th of October, the sessions beginning, I found there was not a moment to be lost; and the affair of Jonathan Wild's throat, together with the business of the Old Bailey, having sufficiently engaged the attention of the keepers, I thought then was the time to make a push.

"On Thursday the 15th, (as near as I can remember,) just before three in the afternoon, I went to work, taking off first my handcuffs; next, with main strength, I twisted a small link of the chain between my legs asunder, and the broken pieces proved extremely useful to me in my design; the feet-locks I drew up to the calves of my legs, first taking off my stockings, and with my garters made them fast to my body to prevent their jingling.

"I then proceeded to make a hole in the chimney of the Castle, three feet wide, and six feet high from the floor; and with the help of the broken links aforesaid, wrenched an iron bar out of the chimney, of about two feet and a half in length, and an inch square; a most notable implement. I immediately entered the Red Room directly over the Castle, where some of the Preston rebels had been confined a long time ago; the keepers said the door of which had not been unlocked for seven years; but I intended not to be seven years in opening it, if they had.

"I went to work upon the nut of the lock, and with little difficulty got it off, and made the door fly before me; in this room I found a large nail, which proved of great use in my farther progress. The door of the entry between the Red Room and the chapel proved a hard task, it being a laborious piece of work, for here I was obliged so break away the wall and dislodge the bolt which was fastened on the other side. This occasioned a noise, and I was fearful of being heard by the master-side debtors Being got into the chapel I climbed over the iron spikes, and with much ease broke one of them off for my purpose, and opened the door on the inside.

"I stripped the nut from off the lock of the door going out of the chapel to the leads, as I had done before to that of the Red Room, and then got into the entry, between the chapel and the leads, and came to another strong door, which being fastened by a very strong lock, there I had like to have stopped; and it being quite dark, my spirits began to fail me, as greatly doubting of succeeding; but cheering up, I wrought with great diligence, and in less than half an hour, with the main help of the nail from the Red Room, and the spike from the chapel, wrenched the box off, and so made it my humble servant.

"A little farther on my passage another stout door stood in my way; and this was a difficulty with a witness, being guarded with more bolts, bars, and locks than any I had hitherto met with. I had, by this time, great encouragement, as hoping soon to be rewarded for all my toil and labour. The clock at St. Sepulchre's was then going the eighth hour, and this proved a very useful hint to me soon after. I went first upon the box and the nut, but found labour in vain, and then proceeded to attack the fillet of the door; this succeeded beyond expectation; for the box of the lock came off with it from the main post. I found my work was near finished, and that my fate would soon be determined.

"I now got to a door opening to the lower leads, which being only bolted on the inside, I opened with ease, and then climbed from the top of it to the higher leads, and went over the wall. I saw the streets lighted, the shops being still open, and therefore began to consider what was necessary to be farther done, as knowing that the smallest accident would spoil the whole workmanship: I was, therefore, doubtful on which of the houses I should alight. I found I must go back for the blanket, which had been my covering of nights in the castle, which I accordingly did, and endeavoured to fasten my stockings and that together, to shorten my descent, but wanted necessaries so to do, and was, therefore, forced to make use of the blanket alone. I fixed the same with the chapel-spike into the wall of Newgate, and dropt from it on the turner's leads, a house adjoining to the prison; it was then nine o'clock, and the shops not shut in.

"It fortunately happened that the garret door on the leads was open. I then resolved at all hazards to follow on, and slip down stairs, but made a stumble against a chamber-door. I was instantly in the entry, and out at the street-door, which I was so unmannerly as not to shut after me, and I was once more, contrary to my expectation, and that of all mankind, a free man.

"I passed directly by St. Sepulchre's watchhouse, bidding them good morrow, it being after twelve, and down Snow-hill, up Holborn, leaving St. Andrew's watch on my left, and then again passed the watchhouse at Holborn-bars, and made down Gray's-inn-lane into the fields—and, at two in the morning, came to Tottenham-court, and there got into an old house in the fields, where cows had sometimes been kept, and laid me down to rest, and slept well for three hours. My legs were very much swelled and bruised, which gave me great uneasiness; and, still having my fetters on, I dreaded the approach of day, fearing that then I should be discovered. I began to examine my pockets, and found myself master of between 40 and 50s. I had no friend in the world that I could send to, or trust with my condition. About seven on Friday morning it began raining, and continued so the whole day, inasmuch that not one creature was seen in the fields: I would freely have parted with my right hand for a hammer, a chisel, and a punch. I kept snug in my retreat till the evening, when, after dark, I ventured into

Tottenham, and got to a little blind chandler's shop, and there furnished myself with cheese, bread, and small beer, and other necessaries, hiding my irons with my great coat as much as possible. I asked the woman for a hammer, but there was none to be had; so I went very quietly back to my dormitory, and rested pretty well that night, and continued there till Saturday. At night I went again to the chandler's shop, and got provisions, and slept till about six the next day, which being Sunday, I began with a stone to batter the basils of the fetters, in order to beat them into a large oval, and then to slip my heels through. In the afternoon the master of the shed came in, and seeing my irons, asked me, 'For God's sake who are you?' I told him, 'An unfortunate young man, who had been sent to Bridewell about a bastard child, as not being able to give security to the parish, and had made my escape.' The man replied, 'If that be the case, it was a small fault indeed, for he had been guilty of the same himself formerly;' and withal said, 'however, he did not like my looks, and cared not how soon I was gone.'

"The next day I took shelter at an alehouse of little or no trade in Rupert-street, near Piccadilly. The woman and I discoursed much about Sheppard. I assured her it was impossible for him to escape out of the kingdom, and that the keepers would have him again in a few days. The woman wished a curse might fall on those who should betray him. I continued there till the evening, when I stepped towards the Haymarket, and mixed with a crowd round two ballad-singers, the subject being concerning Sheppard; and I remember the company was very merry about the matter.

"On Tuesday, I hired a garret for my lodgings, at a poor house in Newport-market, and sent for a sober, steady young woman, who, for a long time past, had been the real mistress of my affections, who came and rendered me all the assistance she was capable of affording. I made her the messenger to my mother, who lodged in Clare-street; she likewise visited me in a day or two after, begging, on her bended knees, that I would make the best of my way out of the kingdom, which I faithfully promised, but I cannot say it was my intention heartily so to do.

"I was oftentimes in Spitalfields, Drury-lane, Parker's-lane, St. Thomas-Street, &c. these having been the chief scenes of my rambles and pleasures.

"I had once formed a design to have opened a shop or two in Monmouth-street, for some necessaries, but let that drop, and came to a resolution of breaking open the house of the two Mr. Rawlings', brothers, and pawnbrokers in Drury-lane; which accordingly I put into practice, and succeeded, they both hearing me rifling their goods as they lay in bed together in the next room; and, though there were none to assist me, I pretended there was by loudly giving out directions for shooting the first person through the head that presumed to stir, which effectually quieted them, while I carried off my booty; with part thereof, on the fatal Saturday following, being the 31st of October, I made an extraordinary appearance; and, from a carpenter and butcher, was now transformed into a perfect gentleman; and, in company with my sweetheart aforesaid, and another young woman, her acquaintance, went into the City, and were very merry together, at a publichouse not far from the place of my old confinement.

"At four in the afternoon, we all passed under Newgate in a hackney coach, the windows drawn up; and, in the evening, I sent for my mother to the Sheers ale-house, in Maypole Alley, near Clare Market, and with her drank three quarterns of brandy; and, after leaving her, I drank in one place or other about that neighbourhood, all the evening, till the hour of twelve, having been seen and known by many of my acquaintance, all of them cautioning me, and wondering at my presumption to appear in that manner.

"At length, my senses were quite overcome with the quantity and variety of the liquors I had all the day been drinking, which paved the way for my fate to meet me; and when apprehended, I do protest I was altogether incapable of resisting; I scarce knew what they they were doing to me, and had but two second-hand pistols, scarce worth carrying about me.

"A clear and ample account I have now given of the most material transactions of my life, and do hope the same will prove a warning to all young men.

"There nothing now remains but to return my hearty thanks to the Rev. Dr. Bennett, the Rev. Mr. Burney, the Rev. Mr. Wagstaff, the Rev. Mr. Hawkins, the Rev. Mr. Flood, and the Rev. Mr. Edwards, for their charitable visits and assistance to me; as also my thanks to those worthy gentlemen who so generously contributed towards my support in prison.

"I hope none will be so cruel as to reflect on my poor distressed mother, the unhappy parent of two miserable wretches, myself and brother; the last gone to America for his crimes, and myself going to the grave for mine.

I beseech the Supreme Being to pardon my numberless and enormous crimes, and to have mercy on my poor departing soul.

JOHN SHEPPARD."

Middle stone room,
Newgate, Nov. 10th, 1724.

" P. S. After I had escaped from the castle, concluding that Blueskin would have been decreed for death, I did fully purpose to have gone and cut down the gallows the night before his execution."

Thomas White, Printer, 59, Wych Street, Strand.